FAKE FIANCÉ

JESSA JAMES

FAKE FIANCÉ

Bad Boys With Big Sticks, Book 1

**By
Jessa James**

Fake Fiancé: Copyright © 2017 by Orange Poodle LLC
ISBN: 978-1-7959-0198-7

All Rights Reserved. No part of this book may be reproduced or transmitted in any form or by any means, electrical, digital or mechanical including but not limited to photocopying, recording, scanning or by any type of data storage and retrieval system without express, written permission from the publisher.
Published by Orange Poodle LLC
James, Jessa
Fake Fiancé

Cover design copyright 2017 by Orange Poodle LLC
Images/Photo Credit: Graphic Stock

Publisher's Note:

This book was written for an adult audience. The book may contain explicit sexual content. Sexual activities included in this book are strictly fantasies intended for adults and any activities or risks taken by fictional characters within the story are neither endorsed nor encouraged by the author or publisher.

This book has been previously published.

1

CHLOE

As Blake Collins walked into the room I took a close look at him. He had a defiant swagger in his step and a determined look in his eyes. The man was drop dead gorgeous. I'd seen him on TV, but never in person. Never when he wasn't on for the cameras, whether on the ice or off. I could tell he didn't care for meetings, and especially didn't like being summoned to one, like some kid to the principal's office.

But rich playboy looked good on him, and I wasn't immune, no matter how much I pretended to be. Everything about him made me want to touch, from the slight wave in his hair, the well-groomed beard he kept just long enough to make me wonder what it would feel like brushing over my inner thighs, to the designer clothes and Italian shoes. Player. Bad boy.

Trouble.

His presence matched his persona, so predictably that I had to smile.

"Blake, this is Chloe Hansen," Frank Stell said, glancing at me, then the others in the room. Frank was my boss and ran the whole West Coast division of SportsAds. And he'd already agreed to my plan...we just hadn't filled lover boy in on the details yet. Frank gave me a look that screamed—I hope you know what you're doing—before turning back to Blake. "You know the others."

The *others* were Tom Lassiter, the white-haired owner of the Detroit Blizzards, some soft young man with glasses that reeked of lawyer, and Ralph Dodge, a sports agent and an all-around decent guy—from what I'd heard—which was probably one of the reasons he couldn't control his client.

Blake ignored the men and turned to me. His wide grin and deep green gaze captivated me as he shook my hand. It was a strong grip, warm and confident. An electric jolt ran through my bones as his skin contacted mine for the first time. He let his eyes run over my body in a practiced glance, the kind that a man gives a woman at a bar, not in a conference room; exactly what I expected from him. Real bad boys played true to form and I grew more confident as he acted like he was reading off a cue card. Frank rolled his eyes behind Blake's back and I smiled, a genuine, full mega-watt smile. I didn't need Blake to like me. Nor did I need to like him. He just had to listen, and my certainty grew to a rock solid knowing in my chest. Blake was going to go along with my plan. He had no choice. He might be a bad boy, but he wasn't stupid. Far from it.

He took a seat across the room, leaning back and turning his attention to the men in suits. I used the opportunity to let my eyes move up, down and over him. His tall and muscular build, the perfected form of an elite athlete that usually lay well hidden beneath his hockey pads. His chiseled facial features gave him an irresistible, rugged look. I had to stop myself from wondering what his skin tasted like, even as ludicrous as it sounded. He flashed a quick smile in my direction, as though he could sense my roaming eyes, showing his perfect white teeth.

This was a business meeting, not a bar pick-up. I shook my head and looked away, irritated with myself for letting a guy like him get me distracted.

This was a job. *He* was the job.

Although easy to look at, my interest in Blake was professional. I already knew the purpose of the meeting. That luxury gave me the chance to turn my attention to his reactions as he got his ass chewed out. The team boss gave him an ultimatum. I could tell by the way he held himself that what they were saying did not make Blake a happy man—I watched his posture change as their words sank in.

"What do you expect me to do?" he demanded, sitting up, his casual demeanor and cocky smile gone. "Pretend to be someone else? Hide in my house?"

I crossed my arms, my smile back. Even if I hadn't known his reputation as a bad boy, the tone of his voice was proof enough. Blake always got his own way and expected it would stay that way. The hockey star needed to change and he didn't like it one little bit.

Better get used to it, Blake.

Seeing him squirm amused me. A satisfying vindication washed over me as I watched the shit show play out right in front of me. I lived for bearing first hand witness to unfolding drama. Cleaning up celebrity public relations disasters was what I did. The challenge Blake presented brought a different kind of excitement to the job. Blake Collins, always in control, always perfect for the cameras, appeared to falter when the word *fiancée* came up.

I knew I'd do my part to keep him uncomfortable for some time and a part of me enjoyed that. When I dealt with macho guys who thought being tough meant they should always get their way, the challenge to see if I could get them to bend, even a little, was intoxicating. There was nothing I loved more in the world than an alpha male. Hot. Dominant. Confident. Most of the posers in the celebrity world folded when the pressure got too high. But Blake?

He was cornered, but he wasn't down. The fire burning in his eyes made my heart race. God, I'd bet he was incredible in bed.

His gaze darted to mine and the heat there made me forget to breathe. We stared for long seconds and I couldn't stop wondering what kind of lover he'd be. Guys like him usually went to one extreme or the other. They either took what they wanted and didn't care much whether or not their woman enjoyed the ride…or they prided themselves on breaking a woman into pieces, devouring her until she was wrung out on pleasure and totally under their command.

My panties grew wet and my nipples hardened beneath my blouse. Thank goodness I'd worn the thick push up bra today. I was giving nothing away, showing no weakness. Not to a predator like him.

Having the tables turned on guys like Blake always got them worked up. I could feel his frustration, and that just added more fuel to my fire, provided the extra spark and drive I would need to hold up my end of the bargain. It made my job all the sweeter.

I couldn't change him, of course. I knew that. A leopard didn't change his spots, or whatever. Blake might play along and follow orders and pretend for a time, if the stakes were high enough. He'd behave while the pressure was on, but he wouldn't accept this as the new normal. Bad boys always reverted. When the shackles come off a couple months from now, there would be fireworks. He'd probably party for a month straight and fuck a new woman every night. It was in his DNA.

Fortunately, what might happen after this job didn't

concern me. I just needed to put him through his paces for a time. I'd be well paid for the effort, and I looked forward to seeing him squirm. I could even argue that it was for his own good.

Blake happened to be a star hockey player. He was thirty-two and, in my opinion, peaking. Total man-candy. He was big and rough and self-assured—too much so. His physical strength, skills in playing the game, and bad boy attitude had taken him to the top. At six-foot-two, two hundred and ten pounds, Blake played an aggressive left wing for the Detroit Blizzards. He'd earned a reputation for mixing things up on the ice in a seriously physical way. He'd become the enforcer on the squad. His brutal forechecks rattled the opposition and had played a significant role in putting the team into the final best-of-seven round of the playoffs against Winnipeg, which were about to start.

Blake's rough style of play also made sure the penalty box didn't stay empty. Not that he got thrown in there more than others, but he had a way of goading the other team into going too far and paying the price.

I didn't consider myself a great hockey fan, but I knew the guy's stats like the back of my hand.

I'd prepared for this job.

Most important, I'd watched videos of his press conferences, spent hours poring over raw material without noticing the time slide by.

And now in this room, in his presence, I understood his reputation as a lady killer. He radiated a sexual heat, even at a distance, and shaking his hand I'd felt a hot longing radiate to my core. I'd love to hear him lean in and whisper dirty words in my ear. Carnal promises. Then fulfill them at the end of the night.

He glanced over at me, and I saw the flick of his tongue, wetting his lips. I imagined that tongue between my legs working my clit and I had to suppress a gasp. I hated myself for falling into his sexual trap for a fleeting second. I refused to squirm, to let him know how affected I was by such a simple gesture.

Idiot! I had to control that kind of response. This stud might be hot and desirable, but he was also an asshole who brought nothing but trouble for himself and his team. I needed to get him on track in public, not in my bed. He was my project. My job. I told myself that it was good to know that I found him so damn attractive. If I stayed aware of it, I could watch myself. Keep my walls up, and the batteries in my vibrator fully charged.

He's an asshole, I reminded myself, as if that made him less hot. I blew out a deep breath, trying to regain my mental composure.

"We've said our piece," Tom Lassiter said, putting his hands on the table and standing. The lawyer jumped to his feet and Tom nodded toward me. "As the head PR rep of this little project, Chloe has developed the strategy. She's in charge and will tell you what you need to do."

"Wait," Blake said, holding up his hand. "What, exactly, am I supposed to do?"

Tom smiled. "Blake, you do whatever the fuck she tells you. This is her specialty. All I care about is results." He narrowed his gaze, all rainbows and unicorns were gone. "I expect you to cooperate with her."

The men left with an "or else" hanging in the air.

Blake turned to me and blinked. "You?"

"Me. The name's Chloe," I reminded him.

"You're going to fix what ails me?"

I laughed. "I'm going to fix what is *failing* you—your image."

He snorted. "And you can do that?"

"Actually, you have to do it." I pointed at him. "You're a

mess, Blake. And if you don't clean up your image, you're going to get traded to a losing team. After that, watch all your endorsement deals dry up like mist in a desert."

His gaze was so intense, I could barely breathe. "Fuck you, Chloe."

I'd expected that, the crude words, the tough guy behavior meant to test me, to knock me off balance. But I was not a little girl to be intimidated. I had the upper hand here, and we both knew it. "Not even on a bet, Blake."

Ralph Dodge sighed and put his hand on Blake's shoulder, taking his turn to reassure this grown man who, even in his thirties, appeared to need a whole bunch of coddling. "You want the team to renew your contract, right? You want me to score that endorsement deal I've been whispering about? Well, son, both of those are within reach, but they're hanging by a thread. No one wants to put your face all over their promo and then have you shit on them by getting busted for a DUI or showing up in tabloids naked at some pool party orgy."

Blake flinched and turned away as his face reddened.

I had to smile. Neither example was hypothetical. Blake was known as a party animal—a work-hard, play-hard sort of guy. But the good times had caught up with him. A week prior he'd gotten caught up in a drug bust at one of those parties and that had tipped the scales. The team was making calls, talking trade. It was only a matter of time before it leaked to the press.

"Look, Ralph," Blake began. I recognized the tone. "First thing is, don't call me son. Second is, I'm killing it on the ice. We're in the playoffs with a good chance of winning. Why does the team give a fuck about my private life?"

"Because it's not private, Blake." I held up my cell phone where I had an image from my feed featuring his mug shot from the other night. "It's public, and loud, and making your team look bad."

"I had nothing to do with what happened at that party. I like women. I admit it. But I don't do drugs, and I sure as hell don't deal them."

Roger cleared his throat. "We know. But Frank Stell's agency is connected to a lot of big corporate players, and he doesn't like the message your behavior is sending. Didn't you hear Frank talk about the trend to make hockey a more family-oriented sport? It's not just you, and it's not just the Blizzards."

I watched a smile spread over Blake's face, a cocky smile, one that got women to drop their panties and men to change their minds on deals. "So, they want me not to party so wild? I can do that." He glanced at me. "I don't need a PR lady to do that."

"They expect you to rehabilitate your image and they're giving you thirty days."

He frowned. "What the fuck does that mean, Ralph?"

Ralph sighed. "They want to see that you've matured, found a new, more wholesome path."

"They want you to show them that being a barbarian on the ice doesn't have to mean a life of sex, drugs, and rock and roll," I added as I linked my fingers together on the table. "They want players to be more civic-minded these days, to set a good example for the young players. They want mom and dad to pay two hundred for a ticket so little Johnny can come watch you play and get an autograph."

He laughed. "How am I supposed to reinvent myself in a month? Find religion?"

"That would work," I replied. He looked shocked for a second. "It doesn't need to be that extreme, but we do need to convince the world you think there's more to life than partying."

I moved to sit on the table and position myself above the superstar. "If you aren't ready to join a church just yet, then I have another plan."

A knowing half grin spread across his face and he shook his head as he leaned back in his chair. "You think you have a plan?"

"One that will show them that you're a bad boy who's decided there are some limits."

"I hope it's better than the plan you're working at right now." Blake stared intensely into my eyes and I could feel the heat of his gaze. "And who exactly are you again?"

"A specialist in handling asshole macho celebs who've fucked up their public image and need to fix it quickly."

"Right." He moved to stand. "Well, thanks for the thought, but I already have a coach on the team. Why should I let you write the playbook for my off-time?"

"Do you want to play hockey for the Blizzards next season, Blake?" Ralph asked. "I want you to. But your contract is up and management is deadly serious about this."

He puffed his chest and pointed at Ralph. "This is my team, I hold this franchise together. Did you lose count of how many times I've been MVP?

Ralph tried the father act again. "How well you play the damn game is only part of it now. This team is a business with sponsors and investors. The city and state political types need to be made happy, too. You, behaving like a juvenile delinquent, needing favors from the cops so often... those things make it harder to get what the team wants. They wonder if you'll be in jail when they need you and the sponsors start to balk. That's when they look at your contract renewal and think of all the other players who might work better for them—even if they aren't as good at left wing, maybe they're damn close. And maybe they're better for the team off the ice."

Blake sagged down into the chair and glared at me as if this was my doing. "So, I'm fucked?"

I sighed. "Not if you do what I say. There are three months until your contract expires so we have time to clean you up. As long as we make good progress in the first thirty days, we can do this."

"And that means what?" He turned to gaze out the office window.

"There's only one thing, one believable thing, that could happen to make a bad boy straighten up in the public eye… something that might give you a reason to change." I let him wait a beat before dropping the bombshell. "True love."

"What?" He looked at Ralph, shocked, as though I'd just told him he needed to become a monk in a traveling circus.

"Blake, you're going to get engaged."

The look on his face changed to horrified as he turned toward me. "Why would I do that?"

"Because fairy tales always sell."

"Sell?"

"We want the public to buy your story. While partying and living his blessed life, Blake Collins met a girl and finally fell in love. You met her and now you're so crazy for her you decided to quit chasing tail and settle down. You've reformed. Been redeemed. Will do anything to make her happy."

He put his hand to his chest. "Me?"

I smiled and pointed. "You, Blake."

"Congratulations, son," Ralph said, chuckling.

He was stunned. "Engaged? To who?"

"We make it news. You'll make appearances with your fiancée, be seen out on the town. You can go to parties, saner ones than your normal, but she stays by your side and you pretend you love your new life and wouldn't do anything to hurt her."

"So, I have to get married to play hockey happily ever after?"

"This is just a story for the press, Blake." It surprised me that he didn't get it. "It's a three-month fairytale episode in the life of Blake Collins. We announce the engagement and you play the loving fiancé for three months. Once the contracts are signed, you can stage a break-up. You can dump her, she can dump you…it doesn't matter and won't be my problem."

"And this will work? Love conquers the bad boy?" His tone was incredulous.

"Right. She loves that he's a brute on the ice and a cuddly teddy bear in the bedroom—just for her." I batted my eyes at him to make sure he knew I was making my point.

He nodded, although most likely not out of agreement. "And who am I supposed to be in love with?"

"We need someone to play a public role. My company will hire an actress who will do it because it will make her famous."

"An actress?"

"For this to be believable the woman needs to be hot—hotter than or at least as hot the girls you're normally seen with—but she has to follow my script. I'll work with her and create her story of how you two met and all that."

"But we don't get married?"

"No. It's a game, Blake. Just keep up the pretense that you're totally in love and have settled down until after the playoffs and you'll have done your part. After that you can do what you like. Marry her, break up…we can spin it however you like. The message will have taken and will carry over into the off-season."

Ralph grinned. "See, Blake? This lady's the expert. Play along for three months and by then we'll have both a multiyear contract with the team and the product endorsements. And one endorsement leads to others, etcetera and so on."

"And I can be myself again?"

I sighed. "I don't care what you do after that, Blake. You won't be my concern."

Blake sat back and folded his arms. The look he gave me shifted. When I first walked into this conference room he'd been checking me out, letting me know that he wasn't going to pretend not to stare at my ass, legs and breasts. Something had changed but I couldn't decipher what churned behind those eyes. I did have the upper hand, I knew I did, but this change left me unsettled.

"We convince the world that love changed me. The wild-assed hockey star meets the love of his life and now he's playing by the rules like any pussy-whipped sucker who's afraid the hot chick will dump him if he fools around. That's your fucking plan?" He looked into my eyes, unflinching. It was a challenge.

I nodded once. "A crude way to put it, but yes. That is exactly my plan."

"And people will fall for this shit?"

"It's my job to make sure they do, and if you do what I say, follow my directions, it will work."

He started at my ankles as he ran his eyes over me again and smiled when he reached my eyes. "I get final approval on the woman?"

"Within reason." I returned his stare and maintained my resting bitch face, not about to fail this test and look away first. "I'm going to be arranging the play you'll be acting in and casting the parts. Your fake fiancée will play the role in public only."

Blake broke our staring match and got up from his chair to walk to the window. My office sat on the twenty-first floor of the building and had an impressive view. It gave me a good look at his broad back and I found the way his shoulders seemed wider when he moved rather delicious.

"So, Ralphie, you're telling me that without this crazy stunt, I'm done?"

"Not done for sure, but not on the way up either," Ralph replied. "Without something happening, even if the team renews your contract, it will not be for the money you should get, and forget the endorsements. The market is for athletes who are good role models."

"So, she's worth what I'm going to pay her?" He glanced at me, then back to Ralph.

"I'd say so."

"Do I buy the girl an engagement ring?" He turned and faced me.

"Of course. We could even stage the proposal so that the media are there," I said. "You'll tell her you're giving up other women for her. It will be dramatic."

"Dramatic bullshit," he said. I nodded. "I got where I am by being who I am. I won't change."

He didn't need to tell me that.

"We're just modifying your image. You can still be a tough guy—they want that. Think about the game—you know how to fake it on the ice, like pretending you're tripped or took a high stick. It's bullshit with a purpose."

"I don't like it." He sighed, but the ire was gone from his voice. I had him, I just had to reel him in.

"Understand that in business being a bad boy only takes you so far. You're at the top of your game. Staying there will mean learning how to play the game both on and off the ice. You need some new skills and I can teach them to you."

He tipped his head, looking at me. "You want this gig, don't you? It would be another feather in your cap."

And money in the bank. "Sure. It's my job. This is what I do."

"Then we'll do it together."

"Of course."

"I mean really together."

I caught a devious sparkle in his eyes. "What are you saying?"

"I'll follow your game plan, do what you say, but only if you become a player-coach."

"I still don't get it. Try it again in English."

The cocky grin was back. "I want you to be my fake fiancée."

2

BLAKE

I rather enjoyed the look on Chloe's face when I insisted she play the role of my fiancée. She was sexy-as-fuck and the dumb jock had surprised her. Of course, then she'd surprised me right back by agreeing and here I'd just been yanking her chain. She called my bluff and now I had to go along with it. Go with her.

I didn't like the plan at all, but given that the team owner and the companies with the bucks for endorsements all had their minds set that we needed to create a brand new and improved Blake Collins, I didn't have much leverage.

At least this Chloe presented a challenge—a lovely, leggy challenge who didn't seem to fall for my charms in the slightest. In fact, I was pretty sure she didn't even like me. She looked at me with a thin smile that said *You're just a client*, not the millionaire hockey player with expert moves on and off the ice.

Wanting to wipe that smug look from her face had been my half-assed reason for insisting she play the girlfriend. No, fiancée. Now, since the game was on, I'd have time to make her mine. It didn't seem like a bad plan; guaranteed access to a gorgeous woman that I'd wanted from the moment I first shook her hand.

I didn't date professional women and damn sure never planned to make one my fiancée, but if I could get her to spread her legs for me I bet I would be in for a wild ride. She'd give as good as I gave her. She'd be passionate, wild. Hell, beneath that prim suit her body curved in luscious directions. And if I had to play this stupid game, then I could use the time to get to her, break down her resistance, strip off that trim pencil skirt and modest blouse. I imagined having her beg me to fuck her. Only then would I.

I shifted, trying to hide my growing hard-on.

She agreed to the job and moved toward the door. "We can start right away."

"Now?" I hadn't expected her to be quite such a ball buster. Yeah, she needed to chill the fuck out and a few orgasms would help with that. It would be so much fun to see her all sated and sweaty from my fingers, my mouth. My cock.

"Tonight," she said, breaking me from my lusty thoughts. "If you have anything planned, cancel it. You're taking me out to dinner. We've met and had an instant rapport. We'll be seen a few times and then Saturday I'll be at the game and we'll go out after." She frowned. "Next week you'll buy me a ring and we'll make an announcement."

"That fast? I might have you in my bed. That would be believable, but a ring? That quickly?"

I saw her blush and had to wonder how far down beneath her blouse it crept. "We can't see how well it's working until after an official announcement, and convincing the suits will take time. And you will not have me in your bed."

Ralph nodded. "It needs to be quick."

She shot a look at Ralph. If looks could kill, old Ralphie'd be dead.

"The ring." Ralph stammered. "Not the bed."

She handed me a card. "There's my cell phone number and address. I'll expect you to pick me up at seven."

"Where am I taking you?" I figured, fuck it, she's the pro, let her make the call outside of the sack, but in it, she'd be listening to my commands. No matter how deadly the looks, I will have her. The electricity between us was palpable…and in this area, I was the professional.

"To The Stanley Cup," she said. "You make the reservation."

I laughed. Her choice made sense—the restaurant was owned by Johnny Lance, a former Blizzard. As the restaurant name suggested, it was a hangout for hockey players, team owners, and fans.

Ralph approved. "That will get the word out fast."

She nodded. "To the right crowd."

I stood and looked at Ralph. "I'll do my part, Ralphie, and you do yours." He nodded. "I have some work to do before our date tonight."

"Seven then," she said, holding the door to her office open for me. "Dress nice."

I did have work to do. I went home and called Johnny's restaurant, made a reservation for two, then watched some videos of Winnipeg playing their last two games. Saturday, we were the home team for game one of the playoffs. I studied the moves of my opposite number, looking for body language cues that would tell me what to expect.

But I struggled with distraction, a certain curvy, long legged blonde distraction.

When I turned off the clips—only able to pay partial attention anyway—I made a call. "I won't be over tonight," I told the luscious redhead who answered. "Business problems."

"When will I see you?"

I sighed, thought about the next three months that loomed before me. "I have no idea, but not for a while."

"Asshole!" she said and hung up.

She was nothing but a pretty face, a sexy body and a girl who'd slipped me her phone number. There were plenty of those, but I still felt a twinge. She was a sure thing. But that wasn't part of the plan and I couldn't afford to risk fucking up this very expensive operation. The only woman I could have right now was Chloe and with her cold professional exterior and she appeared to have better defenses than the Winnipeg's back line. I sighed, rose from the couch, stretched and smiled.

I did enjoy a challenge.

3

CHLOE

When I laid out the idea, I should have expected that Blake would dig his heels in and make some sort of unreasonable demand. That was his nature, to be a bad boy who had to make things as hard as possible. He had to act out and be a pain in the ass. He wanted to be in control.

Fortunately, he miscalculated. He'd accidentally come up with what was going to be the very best solution. By spinning the story that he'd fallen in love with his PR person, we started immediately on his image rehabilitation and I had total control. He might have thought he was smart, but I was smarter.

It wouldn't be easy, though. I'd have to spend a lot of time in his smoking-hot company without melting, without ruining every pair of panties I owned. I had no idea how I could feel so much sexual intensity for one person, a complete and total irritating man at that.

After the initial meeting, I'd stayed at the office and made my report. Frank, my fast-paced, driven, exhausting boss had found it hysterical. He survived on black coffee and energy drinks. I respected him and we had a good working relationship, for the most part. I felt as if I had to stretch the truth sometimes to keep him happy, but so far it had worked just fine. And my arrangement with Blake, Frank loved it.

"Marrying the client wasn't exactly the way I understood your plan was supposed to work," he said. "It will simplify the billing though."

"No one will expect us to marry except for the public," I countered. "We don't care what happens after the three months are up."

"You're comfortable playing the fiancée?"

"Sure," I told him. I often lied to my boss. It was efficient, tidy and I had no interest in going back and forth about it, especially with Blake as my fiancé. He wasn't some random guy in trouble with his boss. He had a long trail of women's panties behind him and damn it all, scorching hot looks.

Frank bought the lie, or at least had the good graces to pretend he did. And why not? No matter how I set it up I'd be putting one-hundred percent of my time into this one account until the job was finished. That's how I worked. It was the only way I could do things—focused, either all-in or all-out. Type-A all the way, and I wasn't going to change the way I worked best for anyone. Frank knew that, so he stayed quiet.

"We're having dinner together tonight," I told him, sharing the first part of the plan. "We need to be seen out a few times, then make the announcement this week."

"Before the next game."

"It should be on the news when the potential ad agencies are looking at their options."

He nodded. "Good. It's in your hands. Don't fuck it up."

I didn't intend to, but didn't appreciate his tone with me. I'd realized long ago it was the name of the game. No one ever said it would be easy being successful as a woman in this business.

I tried to balance the girlfriend look with style as I got ready and when Blake showed up his eyes showed he was pleased with my choice.

"You've cleaned up well yourself," I teased and he laughed. At least he had a sense of humor.

The restaurant was nice and, as I'd hoped, we were seen by a lot of the right people. I noticed a social columnist, although I couldn't be sure he'd know who Blake was or thought he was newsworthy, but he'd remember seeing us. A sportswriter for the Chronicle had been at the bar when we came in and he gave us a second look, nudging the guy he sat next to with his elbow, and pointing, probably asking who I was. We were already seeing reactions of this plan, and that was perfect.

We could use all of that we could get.

4

BLAKE

When I picked Chloe up, she'd looked stunning in a slinky, sparkly black dress that made it impossible to ignore her luscious curves. My cock had pulsed behind my dress pants. He certainly approved. Her blonde hair hung loose down past her shoulders, framing her face and I itched to run my fingers through it. I had no idea how she made it look so wavy and perfect. I pictured myself fucking her from behind while I grabbed a good fist full of it. That train of thought was getting me nowhere, although my cock didn't seem to mind.

"Time to go to work," she'd said, distracting me from my thoughts of fucking her.

Walking beside me to the car, I'd noticed she was taller than most women, but she only came up to my nose, even in heels. A girl with long, slender legs always made my dick hard, and she was no exception.

My heart had begun to race and I felt a rush of heat spread over my body that I wasn't used to having when I was with other women. From what I'd seen of Chloe, she was a spitfire, and I loved the challenge.

Desire had bubbled up inside me as she moved like caramel to get into my sports car. I caught a glimpse of her creamy thighs as she settled down in the seat and had to wonder how soft they'd feel against my lips. I gulped as I suppressed a feeling of longing that overcame me. I wanted her in my bed, her taste on my tongue.

When we were seated at the restaurant, Johnny, the owner, came to our table. I introduced Chloe and he gave her a big smile. "This is my girlfriend," I told him. "Hands off."

His stunned expression said it all. "Girlfriend? As in a girl you can be serious about for more than one night?"

"Looks like," I said. Shit. Why did I feel like such an asshole by his question? And in front of Chloe. She knew I was a man whore, but having Johnny point it out?

He smiled at me. "Keep an eye on this one, sweetheart. You have a real challenge on your hands."

The fucker. It was one thing to have a new girl on my arm every night, it was another for Johnny to make me look like such a dick. I didn't make any promises to any of the women I fucked and was careful to extricate myself before moving on to the next. They knew the score.

I held up a hand. I felt like I needed to explain myself to Chloe, as if I wanted to impress her even if it was all pretend. "This is different, Johnny."

Johnny looked stunned for a moment, then nodded as if he'd heard it all before. As if he didn't believe me. "Like I said, Chloe, good luck with this one." He winked and, thank fuck, walked away.

"He's a hard sell," I told her. Beneath the soft lights of the restaurant, she looked even more beautiful. Full lips, high cheekbones, pale blue eyes. But she had something most of the other women I'd been with didn't. Brains. She was attractive and *smart*.

"You don't have the kind of track record that inspires confidence. Don't worry, I know the score."

For once, I felt a little ashamed of my history with women. I wanted Chloe to like me. Hell, for some reason I wanted her to respect me.

"That's why you're going to have to play it totally straight until people actually believe that you believe it yourself. I don't think it will be easy for you."

She was right. Unless I seriously wooed Chloe Hansen this plan didn't bode well, but if I wanted Tommy to renew my contract I had to play the game. Hockey was the most important thing in the world. The reality was that I could chase pussy or play hockey but not do both.

It was a hell of a choice. She represented the corporate bigwigs and I hated the idea that she might understand my weakness for women. No, she knew it, especially after Johnny's little visit.

I brushed her concern off. "Don't worry about me. You might not know me or believe what you've read about me, but I'll play my part." I felt like I needed to keep up my edge, my tough exterior. I wasn't ready to have any woman, no matter who they were, breaking down my walls.

She studied me for a minute. "All right. I'll believe you. Besides, I've got three months to find out for myself. But this isn't a joke. Once the word is out that you're seeing me, especially after our engagement, the press will be watching us both like hawks. I'm an unknown, and it won't be as intense for me, but they'll be expecting you to backslide. You'll see reporters lurking, waiting to catch you with another woman. No matter how smart you think you are, you can't sneak around and get away with it."

"Despite what you think, I've never cheated on a woman," I emphasized the words clear and slow. "And losing the chance to play hockey isn't worth the risk of shagging some bimbo," I said.

"And it was before now?" she asked.

Good point.

I shrugged. "I'm reformed, remember?"

"Good, but you better be prepared for some of these reporters to try setting you up." She took a sip of her wine.

I frowned. "Set me up how?"

"Any number of ways." She ran her finger over the rim of her glass and I watched the motion. My cock twitched, eager for the same motion over the crown. Good thing I was sitting down. I wouldn't be able to hide my hard-on.

"They might pay a woman to try and get you to cheat on me and when you do…well, if that happens your career is going down the tubes."

Shit. She was right. It may have been the first thing we truly agreed on.

"Game day is the worst," I told her.

She arched one tapered brow. "Why?"

"That's when the women are all over us—the players. They swarm when we leave the security area and go out to the parking garage. They're after autographs, but many want a hot night and the press know it."

Games always got me worked up, and the rougher the game…well, Winnipeg played as hard as we did and that was great for me and the fans. But afterward, I'd want to get laid because the rush hadn't worn off. I'd gotten used to having lots of women around who wanted to oblige and game day was easy pickings. I kept condoms in my locker so I could stuff some in my pocket when I left. I always knew they'd be waiting outside for the team. Some would stuff a phone number in my hand or in my pocket. Many would rub their bodies against me and make wonderful, filthy suggestions.

Giving one of them a call from my car and telling her where to meet me was never a problem.

Some were trouble though.

A few weeks back there'd been a curvy brunette with shoulder-length hair and lush, sensuous lips who'd walked beside me all the way to my car, whispering in my ear that she'd do whatever I wanted right there in the parking garage. I might be a little wild, but I didn't do public fucking, so we'd gone to a party. A wild party the cops busted.

Turned out, the groupie was holding drugs. She'd wanted to go to the party to deal. She got busted and the lot of us were taken downtown to give a statement. I wasn't charged with anything, but the press got word I'd arrived with the drug-dealing brunette and by reading the tabloids you'd think I'd been convicted of dealing.

That was when I'd learned that the people who signed the checks were more concerned about my image than I'd ever been. That was why they brought in Chloe to act as my keeper.

For tonight, for the next few weeks anyway, that meant being out with her.

"I'll attend every game," she said. "I'll have security let me in to meet you when you come out of the locker room. I'll be with you when you walk to your car. In fact, you won't drive. I'm arranging transportation from now on."

I sighed. That would work…unfortunately. I'd have to pretend that I was going to score with my fiancée, but in truth, there was a chance I'd have blue balls for three months.

Still, I could I let my eyes wander over Chloe's body without harm, and I did now. I tried to snap out of it. I didn't want to appear like I was daydreaming or picturing her naked. I was, but Chloe didn't need to know that. I couldn't get a handle on her yet. I didn't know her hot buttons, but the reality of what I'd agreed to do was sinking in. I couldn't

Fake Fiancé

imagine not playing for the Blizzards, not having my contract renewed. Tom knew I'd do anything to make that happen. But I hated that Chloe was running the show and had me by the balls.

All eyes would be on me and I didn't have any leeway to screw up. This was my one chance not to fuck it up. I'd gotten myself into this mess and I had to do as Chloe said to get myself out of it. The thought made me sweat. I had so much riding on whether this worked. I just hoped Chloe knew what she was doing. She claimed to be the best at her trade, and I was ready to see her in action.

While I was tense throughout dinner, she acted totally at ease. I just had to wait and vent my frustrations and pound my aggressions out on other people. On the ice. It was one of the only jobs where that type of behavior was actually acceptable. That paid me the big bucks.

We were interrupted a couple of times during dinner, first by Randall, a teammate who wanted to meet Chloe. Randall played right wing. He was good, but I couldn't say I liked him. Even more, I didn't like the way he looked at Chloe, like he thought she was completely fuckable and wasting her time on me.

"You're out of your league, Blake," Randall, whispered as he left. "You should hand off the play."

"Fuck off," I replied. My blood boiled but I bit my tongue and kept my cool, even though it was eating me alive to do so.

Chloe heard him. That knowing smile was back on her pretty face. I watched the glow of her blue eyes and saw that she met my gaze levelly. Her self-confidence made her even hotter and I looked her over again, letting my eyes savor the curves of the bare tops of her breasts that her low-cut dress showed teasingly. Fortunately, I knew Randall wouldn't have a shot with

Chloe since she was busy being my fiancée for the next three months. My cock pulsed knowing no one else would have her.

Next over was Bert Walker, who wrote a column for the Chronicle. He was a sports writer, but he mostly wrote gossip. He liked to cover the scene, writing about contracts and business shit. That was his excuse for coming by, but there was going to be a piece about my date in the next edition instead, I was sure. "So, I guess Tom isn't thrilled about your recent publicity," he said, not even introducing himself. I had to do it for him. The dude had never been good with subtlety.

"He's over the moon about it. It's attention, Bert."

"Nothing he can sell in this market, Blake. It's a new age, era of the corporate, polished superstar, wouldn't you say, Ms. Hansen?"

She smiled. "Mr. Walker, most women will always have a thing for bad boys, even if it's fantasy. Advertisers know that. It might not sell four-wheel drive pickups, but if they want to get to the soccer moms they can't ignore it."

He laughed. "Point taken, Ms. Hansen, point taken." And then, having learned what he wanted to know, or just gotten some quote he could use, he left us.

"Tomorrow's story will be about how the hot PR lady likes bad boys," I told her.

She cocked her head and gave me an amused smile. "That fits our storyline nicely, doesn't it? This dinner is working rather well."

I watched the rise and fall of those lovely breasts. I wanted to cup them, test their weight, watch as her nipples hardened beneath my thumbs. Suck on them until they were cherry red and she was close to coming.

I cleared my throat. "So, what happens after dinner?"

"Besides dessert?"

Was she insinuating something? Was that a hint? This girl was fucking with me for sure. I raised an eyebrow at her.

Chloe looked like a decadent, expensive and delicious dessert and I found myself imagining easing that dress down, baring her breasts and letting the slinky dress fall to the floor, leaving her in just her panties and sky high heels. If I got her into bed, so worked up she was begging me to fuck her, maybe I could keep my sanity. It might work out, letting the world think she was leading me around by the nose for a while if I was running things behind closed doors.

She tipped her head. "After dinner you take me home."

I looked at her mouth. Her lips were curled into a cool poise of a half smile, half smirk. Her face was more relaxed than it had been in the office, more sensual.

"I should go in," I agreed. "If we're supposed to be a couple, I wouldn't just drop you off."

"You wouldn't?" she teased.

"Here we are, in love…damn right I'd go in." I put my forearms on the table, leaned in. "Like you said, you never know if the press will be watching."

"They won't see much through closed blinds." Ah, she wasn't into public sex. That was fine with me. When I got her naked, I didn't want anyone else to see her. Her body, her cries of desire, would be mine.

"They'll see me go in." I shrugged. "If I announced an engagement to a girl they thought I hadn't even slept with… well, we'd be better off trying to convince them I'd gotten religion overnight."

No matter what she did, she couldn't erase my past.

"That's true," she said.

She didn't seem to mind me looking her over or having me in her apartment and I wondered if that was what she had in mind. She was killer smart, but this was a job to her. *I* was a job. Not a one-night-stand. Or a three-month-fling.

"Meeting Randall and the writer was an excellent start. We've established ourselves as a couple and we need to keep it up from now on."

I wanted to tell her the thought that popped into my head: *Around this woman my cock would always be up.*

"So, when we get to my place, you'll come in with me. You should stay a while, probably leave in the early morning."

She wasn't the kind who fucked on the first date. That was obvious. But we had three months. I sipped my wine and wondered if she had some kind of wild streak she kept hidden, maybe I could bring it out into the open once we got to know each other better. She couldn't be an ice queen, not with that body, not with that self-confident smile. All I needed to do was find the key that unlocked her, got me between those luscious thighs. That would at least give me something to do, some kind of desirable goal to chase until the damn contracts were signed.

5

CHLOE

Once back in my apartment, Blake settled on the couch as I got us each a drink. I tried not to show how much my hands were shaking as I gave him his beer. I was feeling surprisingly jittery, unsure of how this night would unfold now that we were back at my place, and alone. Not that I was going to let anything happen. This was work. Nothing more.

"Stay put," I said as I pulled the blinds, making sure to leave them open a crack.

He narrowed his eyes, still not liking taking orders. I'd brought him a beer. "Where are you going?"

"The script calls for me to change into something more comfortable."

"The script?"

"You were right about the press. We already have an audience. I assume it's reporters that followed us from the restaurant. They smell a scoop."

"How would they know anything?" he growled.

"My guess is that as soon as Bert Walker called in his

story he decided to pick up some extra cash by tipping off the tabloids about the all-star hockey player's new girlfriend."

"Son of a bitch!"

I was surprised by his anger. He didn't seem to have a problem with tabloids when he'd been at that party with the drug-dealing brunette.

"Well, more power to him. That was exactly what we wanted. I expected to have more time to prepare, but that's okay." I dared a glance out of the partially opened blinds. I couldn't see anything other than the blanket of nighttime darkness, but I knew they were there and that made my heart race. I was used to writing the script, not being one of the performers, especially with the leading man being a guy like Blake.

He raised his glass. "Well, here's to something more comfortable."

As he leaned back, I went into the bedroom and changed out of my heels and tight dress and into a robe. It didn't show anything, but it was sexy and I had panties on, just in case, although I wasn't sure what I was concerned about. Yes, this was work, but I was a woman. Did I want to impress Blake and not just the media?

When I walked into the living room, I caught a flicker of interest in Blake's face. That irrational, maddening warm feeling between my legs lit me up again. This was annoying. I'd handled bad boys before, but most of them weren't nearly as sexy as they thought and I found them totally resistible. Blake Collins was just as taken with himself, but something about the chemistry between us was dangerous and different. I was drawn to him by some unstoppable force. I wasn't sure if he felt the same connection but I would find out soon enough. The game meant I had to look sexy when I was with him, pay attention to him, be close and generally try to appear smitten…that all added to the real heat I felt and I was afraid that over time my actions would turn into real feelings. I already knew I had lust in the bag, whether I wanted it or not.

Walking into the living room and feeling his eyes on me, I felt naked and exposed. Vulnerable. I took a deep breath and smiled, feeling awkward for the first time since our encounter began.

We were playing roles, but me? I had two. I was sure every actress worth her salt had moments of insecurity while playing a part, or at least that was what I tried to tell myself. I had to make most of the world think I felt for Blake and let lust dictate my actions. I had to make them think he'd bedded me and I'd fallen in love with him.

He had to play his part in that, which probably wasn't too hard since he had women flinging themselves at him all the time. I also had to make Blake think I was only acting when I stared at him with longing and need, that I was solely keeping a professional attitude about him. My mind was playing ping pong with itself over these roles and I was exhausted already—and it was just the first night.

I did want the conceited jerk, but I couldn't afford to let him know. I craved his touch. I hadn't felt that kind of desire for a man in a long time. I hadn't slept with one for over two years, and the last time had been a disaster.

I focused my attention back on the role. Shadows near the window told me that the reporters had discovered the crack in the blinds. As much as their presence outside of my apartment window totally creeped me out and made me feel violated, I had to stay focused here. I knelt on the couch beside Blake and ran my fingers through his soft hair, then looked at the window more obviously and looked shocked.

"Oh my God! People are looking in." I jumped up and ran to the window and closed the blinds completely.

Blake laughed. "Now what?"

I picked up my phone. "I'm going to report a peeping Tom," I said, tugging my robe as closed as possible. "After the police come and we make our statements, you should go home."

He leaned back and I saw the bulge in his pants. "Do I have to?"

It was exactly the right thing to do. I knew it was. But as I called the police and heard them promise to send a car around, I wanted him to grab me and throw me on the floor, yank the panties off my hips and fuck me silly.

Just thinking of it made my knees grow weak.

"Yes, you do," I said, but I was burning to have him inside me. I had to follow the plan, even if I wore the batteries out on my vibrator in the process.

6

BLAKE

"You have a simple part," Chloe had said. "Just suck it up and get it done," was her advice, accompanied by that half smile that I found both infuriated me and turned me on. She didn't like that I had balked at the idea of the press conference to announce our engagement.

"It's making too much of it." I wanted it to seem real. I mean, who the fuck threw a press conference after they got engaged? It just wasn't normal, sports star or not, but apparently my opinion didn't mean shit to Chloe.

She was adamant. "Look, if I was getting engaged to you for real I would insist on a press conference. As your PR person, I'd tell you that love stories are pure gold. As your girlfriend, I'd want to put all those bimbos who chase after you on notice that you are no longer in play."

Ultimately, I had to admit she was right. Still, I walked into the hotel with an uneasy churning in the pit of my stomach that made me feel a lot like I used to just before a game when I was first in the pros.

Okay, I had stage fright. As much as I hated to admit it,

the limelight wasn't exactly my favorite thing. I loved the attention of sexy women, sure, but when it came to the media being in my face all the time, I honestly hated it. I'd gotten into hockey when I was a kid because I loved the game. Sure, I became good enough to make a career out of it. Sure, money and babes were definite perks, but it had never been about the fame.

It wasn't just that I had to talk to the press and would be on camera—I'd done that thousands of times. I didn't ever mind talking to the press about my playing or a specific game, what went right or wrong, and I didn't even mind facing them when I was being bailed out of jail. It came with the territory, and I knew their right to be there. I didn't necessarily *like* it, but I let it roll off my back. The press was like the annoying little brother I never had.

It used to be funny. I'd never done anything illegal and I thought no one would care about the news stories. I'd been wrong, and now I had to care about my image. My *tarnished* image. My career depended on it. I had so many people breathing down my neck to make better choices it had me screaming inside. My exterior had to remain stoic though, no matter what.

I also hated that this press conference was a staged event. While Chloe was right, I did fake it sometimes on the ice, this seemed different. Going in front of the press to announce our fake engagement was taking another step toward convincing the world a new Blake Collins, a phony one had replaced me.

I felt like Chloe had chopped off my balls, and was ready to display them to the whole world as she tossed and twirled them like golden batons or something. I didn't want to be a different person, and I really didn't want my peers and teammates to think I had become pussy whipped. It just didn't fit with my personality.

Fake Fiancé

But my personality seemed to be my biggest problem and we'd started to fix the shit sandwich I'd made and there was no turning back. Not if I wanted to keep playing for a top team. I had nightmares on what would happen if I got traded to some D-list team where I'd never be noticed again and my pay would be sliced dramatically. I shook the thought right out of my head.

In the days leading up to the press conference, I'd taken Chloe out every night to dinner and dancing in prominent spots, introduced her to people and we'd wind up at her place or mine for part of the night. She always insisted on us ending up at our own apartments by morning. Yeah, I'd seen heat in her eyes, but I never knew if it was real or if she was acting. That was the worst. I knew where I stood with every woman on the planet but Chloe. The only woman I could touch without fucking up my entire career.

The day before, we'd gone to a jewelry store and the goddamn press followed. I'd seen the vultures outside as we picked out an engagement ring. I'd looked over my shoulder in annoyance, but Chloe had turned my head back to focus on her. "We must play the part," she'd whispered. I'd wanted to punch a wall. What was real?

Even with all my frustrations and doubts, everything seemed to be going according to Chloe's plan. She was good at her job and seemed to anticipate everything. That was fine, but she kept her distance except when we were supposed to be a *couple in love*. I was going out of my mind.

The woman had written a goddamn script for the press conference. It was just as well. At least I didn't have to dream up some elaborate story myself. It wasn't bad if you believed in fairy tale fantasies. I could see that some people would want to believe it and she kept it simple: When I got in trouble, Ralph hired Chloe to do PR for me and we'd fallen in love at first sight. Now, I was giving up my man whore ways to be with her forever and ever. The press never used the term man whore, but it was implied.

The very best sex was the first time, especially if you had to work for it. Having the same girl over and over again for the rest of my life sounded like a boring nightmare I didn't want to live in reality. Yet I ached to kiss Chloe, to touch her. For real. But Chloe only wanted the world to *think* we were screwing our brains out.

As we played out her script, I intended to implement my variation to the storyline—one that shouldn't alter the outcome in the least. I'd get this woman wanting me enough that I'd get to hear her beg me to fuck her. The image, the idea of it obsessed me. Begging was the only way I knew to get the truth from those full lips. I needed to know when I slid my dick into her that it was real.

But I had to play her game and pretend I was changing first. I couldn't let her see the bad boy was still alive and well or she'd never let her desire show.

"You're on time," she said when I came into the hotel room.

"You sound surprised." I looked at her and liked what I saw. She had it nailed, the fiancée thing, and was wearing a conservative white silk blouse, all buttoned up and a pencil skirt. A conservative outfit, but on her it was hot. I was sure she knew it too, but I tried to act casual, as if I didn't think she looked so damn fuckable that my pulse was racing.

She shrugged. "Maybe I am." She waved her hand and I saw the light flicker off the diamond in the engagement ring that she'd bought with my money.

"That ring makes the story look real enough."

She gave me that knowing smile again and it made me burn. "We have to sell it," she said. Then she nodded toward doors that led into a ballroom. "You ready?"

I moved close to her and put my arm around her. Her

waist was tiny. I wanted to grab it and hold on as she bounced on top of me as she rode my dick. "I better have a practice kiss before we go in there. You wouldn't want us to look awkward for the cameras, as if we'd never kissed before."

I thought she seemed a little flushed, but her voice was steady. "You're right."

She turned up her face and I bent mine down. As our lips touched, I was sure I felt a slight tremble run through her body. I felt a searing heat run through me and I pulled her close, feeling her delicate body warm against mine. There was no way she could miss my cock growing hard. It was a damn pipe beneath my pants. When we broke the kiss, we stayed like that, catching our breaths. I saw something flicker in her eyes—amusement.

She stepped back and looked at me, her eyes on my crotch. "Perfect. Now you look the part of the eager boyfriend," she said.

"Don't pretend I'm the only one who liked that kiss," I said. Yeah, I had to know. Real or pretend?

"What?" Something danced in her eyes.

"Don't deny I don't excite you."

"You're projecting, Blake. And guessing." Her eyes sparkled as she rubbed up against me. "It's all part of the script. If a hot kiss gets you turned on, I'm happy to provide it. You're supposed to get excited when you kiss the girl you love and your fans would be disappointed if you didn't have that big bulge in your pants when you announced our engagement."

She took my hand and led me to the door. Fuck, the woman was tearing me apart one kiss at a time. I just wanted her to be as affected as me. Hell, she couldn't miss how affected I was.

I sensed some emotion underneath her cool control. Her

message, sent in clear signals, was that she wasn't attracted to me—this was business. I got that loud and clear. Maybe she didn't like dumb jocks. Maybe she didn't like macho men. Who the hell knew? Yet I'd felt that tremble when our lips touched and there was nothing fake about that kiss. It was hot. And I was sure she was as turned on as me. I just wished I could slip my fingers beneath her panties to ensure she was as wet as I thought.

But she was so damn stoic about this. If I was going to get what I wanted, I'd have to get her to confront that desire for me, admit that she was attracted. Then I'd have to get her worked up to a point where she'd say it out loud, where she'd unzip my pants and wrap those long fingers around my rock hard cock and beg me to give it to her.

But this wasn't my game, my world. In this hotel, with her setting the rules in the early stages of this farce of an engagement, I was out of my element. I needed to learn, so I'd play along until I could turn the tables on her, even if it meant walking into that press conference with my arm around her body, feeling her heartbeat, and walking stiffly because of a painfully swollen cock that wasn't likely to get any relief soon.

As we entered, Ralph was at the podium. The press, probably twenty people, sat in folding chairs. At the sides and back of the room were television crews with cameras. I thought they all looked bored.

"Nice turnout," Chloe whispered in my ear.

I snorted. "If you say so."

Ralph smiled. "Ladies and gentlemen, Mr. Blake Collins, the star left wing of the Detroit Blizzards would like to make an announcement of a personal nature."

I slipped my arm around Chloe's slender waist and pulled her hips against mine. The contact made that same tingle in my cock come right back, even in front of all these people. I swallowed hard trying to get myself together so that I could get through the press conference without throwing her down, hiking that pencil skirt up to her waist, moving between her legs and screwing the shit out of her in front of everyone.

It was all part of her skills, of course, being that seductive, that hot, turning it on and off the way she did. I knew that, but it was driving me wild.

As the press applauded, she nudged me. "You're on, darling." Her husky voice rippled through me. I wasn't used to the affectionate tone in her voice.

I took a long breath and faced the audience. Press releases Chloe had written were being handed out. They told the story of us falling in love, and gave them Chloe's bio and the date for our wedding—a year out.

"I'd like to thank you for coming today. The details are in the press release and I'll keep this simple. I wanted to announce my engagement to the beautiful and wonderful Chloe Hansen." She smiled and held up the hand with the engagement ring. "Everything else, all you need to know, is in the press release. I simply asked you to be here in person so you could hear the truth from me and meet my lovely fiancée."

Then, as scripted, I turned to her, looked deeply into her eyes and kissed her.

If I'd thought that first kiss backstage had been hot, I'd been mistaken. This blew it away. Her lips parted at the touch of mine and I instinctively explored her mouth with my tongue. I would get away with it because she wouldn't be able to stop me. My hands slid down her back, traced her spine and then caressed her ass through her skirt. I was getting carried away in the heated moment and nearly forgot we were in front of the media. Pulling her against me I felt the warm, soft press of her breasts, the hard points of her nipples. She moved her hips and that warm and delicious body rubbed over my cock.

When the kiss ended, I struggled to breathe.

"Now we escape," she reminded me, her voice breathy. "Don't answer any questions."

She turned, holding my arm and guided me toward the door leading to the parking lot where a waiting limo. A crowd had gathered, mostly women. Women who, in the past, I would have happily fucked.

But that was over and while I was aware the usual horde surrounded us, I didn't really see them. I didn't find it hard to play my role and focus my attention on the hot body that pressed against mine. To the woman whose kiss I could still taste.

I stepped into the limo and slid next to her. Her skirt had pulled up slightly and I was sure the crowd noticed as I put my hand on her thigh. I moved my hand and the touch felt electric. I had to resist the urge to run it up under her skirt. I wanted to slip my fingers under her panties and into what I was certain was an incredibly wet and warm pussy. She blew me a kiss as the driver closed the limo door, then turned her face away.

I continued to watch her and kept my hand where it was knowing that something was changing. The story was the same, but then had come that kiss. I always thought one kiss would be like any other. This one with Chloe? It hadn't been like anything I'd ever experienced before. I wanted more, even if I wasn't sure what that was exactly.

"I think that went pretty well," she said. Even the calmness in her voice excited me. "The news should be all over the major outlets by the time we get to your place."

Her words brought me back to the reality of the moment. Chloe was only my fake fiancée and we'd just finished a show for the press. She wasn't really the girl of my dreams. At least, she wasn't acting as if that kiss had hit her the way it had me. I was slightly disappointed that Chloe wasn't showing the same type of reaction that I felt to that kiss, but there was nothing I could do about it right now.

"The vultures are following."

No, maybe I could. I could give the press a show and find out if Chloe was faking or not. I waited for the reporters' cars to come alongside to take photos. She turned and touched my cheek, and I kissed her. She responded and her mouth opened. Again, I explored it with my tongue and felt the powerful urge to take her right there. I heard a whimper and I knew *that* wasn't for the fucking reporters. No, that sound had been just for me. When we broke the kiss, my heart was pounding, my balls aching for more.

"Perfect," she said.

"Yes," I said, glad to hear her say it. My breath was ragged and I was a fucking mess over a damn kiss.

"With that steamy kiss, we'll be all over the social media," she said.

I felt like I'd been kicked in the gut. The only perfection she noticed was in the execution of her plan. Who the hell had she kissed before that made her able to ignore this one? She hadn't been immune, but she'd shut down all her passion for the job. Was she a fucking robot or something? I had never kissed a woman who afterwards seemed so distant. I ran my hand over my face, then reached down to shift my cock to a more comfortable position.

"And now we really have to play the part. The readers will want to know if this is real, or some sort of con. The press will be on us like white on rice—we need to stick to the script and stay in character."

In character. That sounded bad to me. "The story will fade soon—it isn't such a big deal," I told her.

She shook her head. Her cheeks were flushed, but she seemed…unaffected.

"You still don't get it. The press will not believe you're giving up chasing tail. Your groupies and the press will expect you to stray. After all, you just met a woman, you didn't undergo a personality change. As long as those girls who crowd around you think there's hope, our engagement will be news."

"Really? So, when they see how I behave what happens?"

"You're a bad boy, Blake, and that's part of the appeal. You're a brute on the ice and an effective player, but the brute part is what appeals to people, especially the female fans. Their panties get wet imagining being with you. The story here is that a bad boy is trying to be loyal."

"And do your panties get wet being here with me?"

She blushed at the question. "This isn't real."

That was not the response I wanted, dammit. I sighed. "I'm not sure how an engagement changes my image."

"It shows you're drawing lines. That you're a star player who's growing up. Becoming mature and not acting, in public, like an arrogant prick."

I winced at her calling me an arrogant prick. I had to admit it stung a little, even if it was the truth, at least to those on the outside. It amazed me how many women liked the idea of spreading their legs for an arrogant prick. But Chloe made it sound like the words even tasted bad.

It surprised me that I cared what she thought about me, that her opinion mattered.

Fine. This bad boy would behave, but I'd also make sure I kept Chloe close and that she found out how mature I could be. If that was what it took to get her to beg for it, then I'd bide my time and try not to go crazy.

7

BLAKE

During the rest of the ride I thought about what I was doing. Chloe Hansen was her own women. She was a mystery. I had a powerful hunch she was going to complicate my life. Hell, it already was complicated. A fake engagement?

If she was as hot as I thought, if she was nearly as good in bed as my imagination made her out to be there was a danger —I could get hooked on her and I didn't want that. I'd seen my parents struggle to stay civil to each other, act nice publicly until we kids moved out and they could rip each other apart in court.

My dad had cheated on my mom multiple times. The apple didn't fall far from the tree, and I didn't want to be *that* guy. Sure, it was fun to sleep around and I had no problem admitting it was a pastime of mine. But I wasn't a cheater. Marriage was sacred and I would be faithful to the woman I married. Some day. This was part of the reason why I never wanted to settle down. I didn't want to make the same mistakes my father had made. I learned early on to keep sex fun and avoid a permanent connection.

My life, my success, made it easy to do that. I was young and I had money. Being single, pussy was plentiful and the idea of sticking with one woman made no sense whatsoever.

"What happens now?" I asked her. I was curious how she intended to play this.

"We follow the plan."

We would keep going on as we had although she was signing me up for some public service events and appearing at a fundraiser for a women's shelter. And we'd be seen together at all of it. "I'll be at the game, of course...all of them. From now on, I'm your biggest fan. Tom invited me to be in his box."

And only Ralph Dodge, Tom Lassiter, his lawyer, and Chloe's boss would know this wasn't real. I sure hoped I wouldn't cave or crack under the pressure. This one was going to be hard for me, especially if Chloe kept on with her standoffish vibes towards me.

The press had fallen back. "I guess they got the pictures they wanted." She took my hand off her thigh and put it on my own lap. "When we get to your place, we go inside. After that public kiss the press will expect us to go straight to bed. You running your hand over my ass worked perfectly. The bad boy can't keep his hands off his girl. We wait a while, then order dinner from a takeout place."

"We make them think we've shacked up?" Although secretly I was wishing that we would in real life.

"They'll be certain we've already slept together, but we need to make it seem like we have insane passion. This is supposed to be a new romance," she said. "Young love. And like you said, you're not the kind of guy who proposes and then waits until the honeymoon to bed the bride. They'll assume we can't get enough of each other."

"You'll stay over?" My heart raced thinking about having her in my bed.

She nodded. "I'll leave early in the morning and take a taxi to my place so I can change for work."

"You're going to the office?"

"You're going to practice and team meetings?"

"Of course. There's a game this weekend. Day after tomorrow." In fact, I was pumped for it.

"I have tons of work to do. I'm running your PR. My intern will help. Saturday, I'll be watching, like a good fiancée. Quitting my job isn't part of the engagement plan. If we were to really marry, I wouldn't give up my career and be a stay-at-home wife."

No, she wouldn't. I liked knowing she had a life of her own. Outside interests.

"Tonight, I'll bring a suitcase over."

"You're moving in?" Outside interests, but at the end of the day, she'd come home to me.

She frowned. "That's how they'll expect it to go. Going back and forth all the time... what's the point? We're pretending that the courtship was a secret. Until now."

I chuckled. "This will be cozy."

That was one word for what it would be like when she was in my bed every night.

When we got out at my place I noticed other cars parked along the street. Two others found places to stop so photographers could hop out and scramble to get around us as we walked to the door. I felt a surge of anger at the pricks waiting like vultures for a good story, then quickly changed my tune because this is what we wanted to happen in the first place.

"Care to make a statement, Blake?" a man shouted as he took pictures.

"I just made one," I said as we headed into the house. Boom, chew on that asshole, I thought to myself. The reporters were swarming now, hurling more questions at us both. Chloe never said a word, just smiled and held my arm.

I felt a sense of relief as we closed the door behind us. We could see reporters moving outside the house and I went around closing the blinds. "Good," she said, settling on the couch.

"What now?"

"Since we're home and relieved at letting the world know that we are madly in love, we rush into bed."

"I could handle that," I said. Her lips twisted into a smile. I thought for a second maybe she was enthusiastic about this after all.

"So, we wait a little longer before we order food. Do you like Indian?"

"Not particularly."

"Shame. Chinese? How about pizza?"

I could eat pizza for breakfast, lunch or dinner.

That earned me a shrug as she glanced around. "Where is your bedroom?"

I nodded at a door. "Right through there." I grinned at her but she just rolled her eyes.

"Come on." She got up and walked to the door, going into the room. I followed her watching the swaying of those hips and wondering what she had in mind. I was pretty sure it wouldn't be what I wanted. I licked my lips and tried to use x-ray vision to imagine what that ass looked like naked.

She sat on the bed. I found it irritating how much seeing her on my bed fully dressed aroused me. Being around her constantly would be hell, a torture I wasn't prepared for nor was I used to. Most chicks couldn't keep their hands off my dick for two seconds. I didn't know how to react to a woman who didn't want to throw herself at me the minute she saw me.

"So, we just sit here?" I asked. I thought about how I'd

have to jerk it in the shower later to release some of this sexual tension.

She shook her head. "We have an audience out there and they need some theater so they can jump to the conclusions we want."

"That we're in here humping like crazy."

"They can't just write that we stayed inside. We need to give them a little something."

"You're really doing this one-hundred percent, aren't you?"

"I never do less than that. That isn't how you succeed."

I sat down next to her. Being around her turned me on every time, no matter how I wanted to feel about her, no matter how much I told myself she was trouble. It was almost impossible for me to think of her as I had any other woman I'd brought into my bedroom—or anyone else's bedroom. Chloe was complex, strong and intoxicating. Chloe was different. Part of it was that strength of hers.

Instead of coming between us, it drew me to her. She was, in her own way, a lot like me. She was doing what she loved, doing it very well, and it had taken a toll on her personal life. I could relate and I felt drawn to her because of that similarity we shared. Like me, she didn't seem to have a personal life. She had no time for one. Maybe she enjoyed one-night stands or maybe she just avoided entanglements of any kind. I knew that I'd been around her for days and she never once made or got a personal phone call. She talked to her boss, her intern at the office, to Ralph, and Tom Lassiter…that was it. She'd taken on this role without needing to rearrange anything in her life.

She was making me think about my emotions, instead of just flying blind and not worrying about any ramifications of my actions. I was cautious and wary around her. I still lusted after her, but sitting beside her on my bed I knew that my plan, my intention to get her to beg to have my hard cock inside her, was foolishness. It made no sense.

What did I want?

Amazingly, I wanted her to like me…to think well of me. I felt the need to impress and wow her. I wanted her to care what my image was, and I wanted to make sure she didn't think I was some asshole by the end of all this. Of course, that didn't mean that I didn't still want her to beg me to fuck her. Every time I looked at her, every time she did some simple thing that made me aware of her presence, like clear her throat, a lust rose up in me. And yet… Being alone with a woman and not at least trying something was not my style. But my style had never met Chloe Hansen before.

We sat in silence for a time. I was lost in my thoughts. The afternoon had been exhausting, stressful and my emotions had me confused. Then she smiled. "Have you got a large t-shirt?"

"Sure. What for?"

"If we're supposed to be in here screwing, I want something to wear during dinner. I should let the reporters get a glimpse of me, just a glimpse, wearing nothing but one of your t-shirts. Maybe when dinner arrives and I answer the door—the pizza." She wrinkled her nose.

I smiled. "How about a hockey jersey? It's got my number on it."

"Perfect."

I went to the closet and got one out. She'd definitely thought of everything, no detail of this plan was lost on her. It was foolproof and I admired that.

"You give these to groupies, right?"

I nodded. "Used to be like that." Step one of trying to get her to think better of me.

She laughed. "Before you found true love?"

Fake Fiancé

"Yeah." Somehow that didn't seem as funny at that moment.

"Then it's perfect. The girlfriend usurps the groupie awards." I watched her stand up, holding the shirt. "I better get changed."

I looked at her. She looked at me. It took me a moment to realize what she meant. She had no intention of changing in front of me. "Oh, sorry. I'll be in the living room."

"Give me five minutes," she said. "Then come back."

I felt the ground shifting under my feet. I'd agreed to this charade because it seemed I had no other choice. I'd insisted on her taking the role so that I could fuck her—so I'd get something more than her PR services for making me do this. It was backfiring. Increasingly, she was even more in control, steering things. And I was losing whatever focus I had, just going along...being a good little boy and not even getting upset. It was like being swept up in some powerful current.

It was unsettling.

When I returned precisely five minutes later, I found her standing by the sliding glass doors that led to the patio wearing my shirt. Her clothes were scattered about the room, as if they'd been torn off. The bed was messed up. She looked at me. "Get undressed."

"What?"

"I want you to add your clothes to this mess, and then get on the bed."

"You want me to get naked?"

She laughed. "That's usually how people are when they've taken their clothes off."

There was nothing sexy about the situation. "What's going on?"

"I'm going to open these shades and walk out onto the patio."

I frowned. "You do remember that there are reporters out there?"

"That's the point. I'll wander out and act like they surprised me, caught me off guard and take photos of me following an intimate moment."

"A number of moments, please," I protested.

"They'll be able to confirm their speculations and have salacious photos of us to share with their readers."

"And sexy pictures of me naked in my bedroom with yet another girl helps my image how? Fixing my image is the point, right?" I was angry because she was calling shots that I didn't agree with. And why did I have to be naked and she didn't? It didn't seem fair.

"This is transition. The idea isn't to pretend you've become a neutered choir boy, Blake, just that you found the right girl. I'm not even sure you get that at all." She was right. I didn't get this whole concept and I was growing increasingly frustrated. "You're still a hot, macho hockey player. That part of your image is a keeper. All we're telling them is that the wild partying is over. You've discovered me and true love. We don't want them to think I cut your balls off, just that you are sticking with me. Then you get boring enough to be a role model. That you've got a new girlfriend is nothing, but you being faithful to her is something else. But first they need a little more convincing this is real, especially since I'm a different kind of woman."

"So, you want me to get naked, why?"

I caught an involuntary twitch of her eyebrow. "For the cause."

"The problem is...." I undid my pants and opened them. My hard cock poked out through the fly of my boxers, looking far more hungry than satisfied. She stared right at my dick and I saw her thin, amused smile creep over her face. "...if I'm naked, anyone photographing me is going to see rather clearly that we haven't been fucking."

Her eyes were fixed on my crotch. "I'm aware of the mechanics. I want you to finish undressing and lie on the bed on your side with your back to the door, as if you're asleep. No one will see that thing."

Ouch, she called my dick "that thing." That hurt. I sighed and began undoing my tie and taking off my shirt. I knew for a fact that if at that moment she were to walk over to me and touch my dick, if she were to wrap her long, lovely fingers around it and squeeze, I'd come right on the spot. The thought struck me that having gobs of my cum splattered over the front of that shirt would be even more convincing, but I said nothing. I was doing what I was told.

The contract, I reminded myself.

She was still looking me over when I got on the bed. I felt her gaze on my back. I wanted her to touch me more than I could remember ever wanting anything before, but then lust makes your thoughts more than a little fuzzy. "Show time," she whispered.

8

CHLOE

As I watched Blake get on the bed, I couldn't take my eyes off the way that muscular ass moved. I tried to suppress a sigh. Not only was he physically attractive, in the short time I'd known him I'd had to revise my rather critical opinion about him. I was still attracted to him but now it amazed me to think that I'd seen him as nothing but a bad boy jock. Of course, that was the image he projected. There was more to him than that, and I didn't think he was even aware of his potential. He was different behind closed doors, or maybe he was still just acting the part as he was told.

I couldn't deny I'd been playing a game, getting him naked. It wasn't necessary at all. I was taking advantage of my leverage over him and enjoying the tingle I got from seeing him naked. He was even more of a hunk than I'd thought and being with me had gotten his long, thick cock rigid. I had to admit that made me feel sexy. Staring at it got my pussy wetter than it already was, and I couldn't shake the fantasy of that cock slipping into my tight pussy. I had to force myself to not think what it would be like for him to fuck me, because I didn't want him to know that I desired

Fake Fiancé

him. I had to remain in my part as the dominating one who called the shots.

I wanted him and my mind was in a frenzy over it, because I had to keep my poise and self-control.

I steeled myself to get back to work. We had a job to do. I pulled open the curtains and saw a flurry of motion in the yard.

I heard a whisper from the bed but didn't catch the words. If it were Blake saying that he wanted to fuck me, I might have melted into a puddle right there, I was sure of it. I took a breath and stepped out. It was late afternoon and still light. As I went into the yard, I became surrounded by men and women brandishing cameras and cell phones. I gave them a deer-in-the-headlights look and prayed they bought it. "What the hell are you doing?" I screamed at them. "Get out of here." I raised my arms in the air for added effect.

Several shouted questions at me at once, so I didn't understand what they were asking. It didn't matter. I had no intention of making any sort of statement. Anything I said would be twisted around. Words didn't matter for this. When the time was right, I'd create a forum where I could control the message.

"There he is," a woman said, stepping into the doorway and shooting a picture of Blake. I grabbed her by the shoulders and pushed her away. "This is private property. Leave us alone!" Then I stepped back inside, closing the door and the shades.

"They jumped on it, just like you predicted," he said, sounding impressed.

I leaned against the door, looking at his back. I was trying to come down from that adrenaline. The praise was unexpected and pleased me, but at that moment the only thing I wanted in the entire world was to get on that bed with him. I wanted his hands running over my body. I was dizzy with lust for him that was clouding the job I'd been hired to do.

As he rolled over and faced me, his gorgeous erect cock had the pull of a powerful magnet. I wanted to stare at it, but I couldn't. I wanted to touch it, but I knew that was completely off limits.

"I'll be in the living room. Get some clothes on and come out and we can order food," I said. He started to get up and I turned and forced myself to run away from that gorgeous hunk and walk into the living room. It might have been one of the hardest things I ever had to do in my entire life, to walk away from that gorgeous naked man. I deserved a fucking medal for this amount of self-control.

My plan was working, but unusually for me, that wasn't enough. As I walked away from the bed I half expected that Blake would call me back. He'd call out my name and, in his deep voice, order me to get into his bed. That would've changed everything between us because despite all my instincts, against all professional reason, I would've done it. I wanted the man too damn much.

I couldn't tell him, but if he acted up to his bad boy image, he would get what he seemed to want. I'd let him have me any way he wanted. If only he'd tell me to. Now I understood why he seemed irresistible to all the other women out there.

The silence rang in my ears as I walked into the spacious living room and sat on the couch. I felt almost wounded by the silence, which was worse than if he'd yelled at me instead. The feel of the soft leather was a shock on my bare ass.

He wanted me. I knew he did. And certainly, I'd gotten him aroused. I hadn't planned to, not at first. I'd dreamed up going out on the patio in his shirt, then it was just so delicious to make him strip for me that way. It amazed me that he did it. He fell for my trap and I got to see the goods.

Fake Fiancé

He had to flaunt his rigid cock, of course. He'd wanted to see if he could shock me and pretend he wasn't surprised when I told him to undress.

By being petty, trying to make the macho guy jump through some hoops I could've tipped my hand. He knew it was bogus and probably realized that I wanted him naked for my own reasons. But he'd done what I'd asked. Somehow, he seemed to be thinking of me differently now than when this started, just like I was thinking differently of him.

Things were a bit out of control. I'd wanted him from the beginning, but that public kiss had almost melted me. He hadn't tried to be sexy. He'd been nervous, just like I was. But when our lips touched, when he pulled me against his body, it had been as if everyone in that room and their cameras all disappeared. I'd turned to jelly.

I can lie to myself like that. I'm a good liar.

Seeing him naked yanked my emotions back to those moments—the molten kiss, his hand tantalizingly close to my pussy in the limo and wishing he would move it a little further south and rub me there. Watching his marvelous body turned me on more than I could've believed possible.

And now…I'd been so close to climbing into his bed with him that I was wobbly, unsteady with the heat of desire. The idea of his hands on my bare breasts or ass, his mouth on my pussy had me wanting something I didn't want. Shouldn't want. But I did want it. I wanted him making love to me. I wanted to know the feeling of that thick, swollen cock thrusting inside me.

I told myself that it was just that I was horny—I hadn't slept with a man in two years. I pretended that I was a workaholic, which was true enough, but the reality was that I was picky when it came to men.

And now… what did I know about Blake Collins?

Superficially, I knew almost everything about him and a

lot of it wasn't good. It suggested that even if he fucked me I couldn't expect him to care about me in a real way. All I'd be to him is a one-night stand—a piece of ass. I knew that and it was a measure of my desperation that I was willing to take that. I was willing to settle for having him shove me up against the wall and fuck my brains out. That's how lonely I was. I couldn't expect him to care about me in any capacity. I'd just be another fuck buddy to him, so I was making the right decision by not trying to get him in bed.

He came out wearing sweatpants and a t-shirt.

"Sit beside me," I said, patting the couch cushions.

"I'll get us a beer," he said.

When he returned and handed me one, he sat next to me and I felt the warmth of his body, reminding me that I was naked under that oversized jersey.

He lifted his beer bottle and smiled. There was I hadn't seen before, but I couldn't place it. It was almost congratulatory. "Did you get what you wanted?"

I took a long sip of the cold beer. It helped. "What do you mean?"

"Having me naked."

"It helped the story." And me, I thought, but didn't dare admit that.

"There were a lot of things that would've worked just as well."

I was uncomfortable that I'd been so transparent. "It was more dramatic that way."

He sipped his beer. "You, Chloe, are a liar. And in this case, you aren't even a good liar."

"Okay, I was testing you. I wanted to see if you'd follow my directions even if they meant a woman was making you strip. I wanted to see if you'd handle a role reversal." He slid an arm behind me, held my waist. I knew I should tell him to move it, but the words were frozen in my throat.

"Did I pass?"

I nodded, not sure how to answer. "Seems so."

"Now you're uncomfortable. Feel off balance."

I was more in heat than off balance. I looked at him to see if he was teasing. "Off balance?"

"It surprised you that I didn't jump your bones."

"No."

"It didn't surprise you?"

I trembled and before I could answer his hand was hot, melting hot on my thigh. I was looking at his face and his eyes were boring into mine. He moved close and kissed me. It was the public kiss all over again, with his tongue in my mouth, my brain locked in an agonizing battle over whether to encourage him or shut him down.

The arm around my waist pulled me up onto his lap. My bare ass rubbed over his hard cock through his pants as his hand moved between my legs. I shivered. He broke the kiss and moved to nibble my earlobe. I gasped as his fingers reached my pussy and stroked it with a shockingly delicate touch. I moaned softly as he traced the line of my pussy lips, then worked a finger between them.

"Wet," he breathed into my ear. As if to prove his point his finger moved inside me, spreading my juices around the tender folds. His fingers were electrodes, stimulating me as they danced inside my pussy. His mouth attacked my ear, sucking the earlobe in his mouth, then kissing my neck, tasting the flesh. And all the time he used those thick fingers in my pussy, fucking me with them.

"Oh my God!" I cried because I was coming.

He held me, his face against mine, his hand still between my legs. My breathing calmed slowly and I was limp in his arms, waiting for whatever he'd do next. "I guess we better order that pizza," he said. He put me on the couch and I lay back against the armrest. The shirt was up around my waist and his eyes were on my swollen pussy. "I'll give them a call."

I watched him in wonder. What the hell was he doing? Why didn't he fuck me? Did he just make me come to prove a point that he could switch back to having control over the situation in a blink of an eye? Or in this case, a flick of my clit?

When he put down the phone I stood up, trying to get myself together, trying to think. "I think I'll go now," I told him.

"I thought the young lovers would be screwing most of the night," he said. I heard something odd in his voice.

"You never know what young lovers will do, when it comes to it," I said. I walked into the bedroom to dress and go home. I needed distance.

9

BLAKE

I hated the way we left things. It had torn me up inside to not run up to her and take her in my arms and fuck her right then and there. I hated to see her go, but it was important to make my point, that I could stay focused. I wasn't exactly sure why she'd let me take it that far, and it had taken every bit of strength I had to keep from screwing her. Up until that moment, I had never practiced so much restraint in my entire life, it just wasn't my nature.

But she hadn't asked me for it.

I wasn't sure why I was insisting on that, even at the expense of passing on what I was certain would be an exceptional fuck. Maybe I was angry. The money people were using her to manipulate me, so she was part of that. I resented her using her beauty, her sex appeal as leverage to control me. An internal part of me wanted to get back at her for that. She was being paid to hold me by the balls and I wasn't taking it very well.

I spent the next morning with my trainer, working through my fitness program. The workout helped me release some of the angry torment I was feeling. After that I went to the rink and worked out with the team on some passing drills—basic, but critical stuff. By the end, I was feeling a lot better from all the distractions of the day. I remembered what I really was in all this for, the game. I was on my way home when Chloe called, surging me back into the heat of the other game I was playing. "We're going to an art opening tonight and then out to dinner. I've made reservations in your name."

"What kind of art?"

"For charity," she said, sounding puzzled.

I wanted to laugh. She had no idea what kind of art it was. She'd merely scheduled an event. She wasn't selling herself very well to me as a person who had feelings other than the robotic motions of her job. She told me what time I was supposed to pick her up and what to wear. It was a tux, of course, and it was my job to agree with everything she said through a clinched and forced smile.

I'd wear one for Chloe even though it wouldn't get me laid, but it would keep me on the hockey team. Getting her off had been exciting and thrilling. I'd made the ice queen break down her barriers. She hadn't begged me to do her, but she'd been plenty pleased to have me finger her to a lovely orgasm.

From the gallery, we went to a French restaurant that I enjoyed despite an almost total lack of conversation from my "date." "I thought we were still doing the young lover thing. Shouldn't you at least smile at me once in awhile? They're going to catch on and will stop buying it if we don't make it believable. This is *your* game Chloe, remember?"

"Sorry," she said. "You're right." Then she chatted to me about the art we'd seen as if I remembered any of it, but I pretended to be interested anyway, because I was *good* at holding back my true emotions.

After dinner, we went to my place. While I got out of my

tux and into sweats, she kicked off her heels and turned on the television. She sat in a chair while we watched some movie, barely even looking at each other. At least I was out of that uncomfortable tux. When it was over she got out her phone and announced she was going home. There she went with the robotic nature again. This broad had me so confused. "I'll call a cab," she said.

"And tomorrow?" I asked.

"Game day."

"What's the schedule, boss?"

"What do you normally do?"

"I get there early and spend time getting my head right, then warming up."

"Then I'll go directly there on my own. Take a cab to the arena and I'll meet you outside the locker room."

"Sounds good, ma'am." I said sarcastically.

I walked her to the door when the cab came and made a production of kissing her goodnight. I wasn't doing it for the press either. I needed a fix, I needed to touch her and I needed that kiss to get me through the night.

10

CHLOE

Sitting in the owner's box gave me a false idea of what it was like to go to a hockey game and get the full experience, but nonetheless I was impressed. There I was in a lovely setting, with a wet bar, a buffet of really nice nibbles, and comfortable seating. But the seats below, around the ice were packed with enthusiastic fans, many wearing Blizzard or Winnipeg team jerseys, eagerly waiting for the start of the game. Maybe I could get to have the enhanced experience of the game down there in the trenches with them at some point.

Everyone treated me well and was very polite and friendly. Of course, everyone there but Tom Lassiter, the owner, thought I was Blake's fiancée. Tom knew the score, but I had to wonder what he might think if he knew how I was starting to feel about Blake. The game we were playing, creating the story about being engaged was taking me, at least, onto slippery ice. He gave me curious looks at times, almost as if he didn't believe I could pull all of this off.

His daughter Daphne, who was eighteen, introduced

Fake Fiancé

herself and took a seat next to me. A waiter brought a mimosa and a plate of cheese and crackers. I looked down at the rink where the players were warming up, skating around, taking a few practice shots. We had a great view of it all from comfortable seats, plus there were large screens that showed close-ups of the action.

"Elegant," I said. "I could get used to this." I took a swig of the mimosa and let the alcohol sink into my veins.

Daphne chuckled. "The action is better down behind the boards."

I looked at Daphne closely. She was a slender young blonde with unusual dark eyes and a marvelous face—the kind of girl that became more beautiful as she matured.

"Is this normal?" I asked her, referring to his adrenaline pumped fan club.

"It is when Blake's playing," she said and curled her lips up in a half smile as we watched a girl throw what I was certain was a pair of panties at Blake. He casually used his hockey stick to push them over to the side where a referee picked them up and stuffed them in his pocket, as if he was used to that type of thing happening all the time. I was perplexed.

Daphne leaned over. "I think Blake will be a great husband."

"Really? With his reputation, most people have been telling me what a mistake I'm making." Daphne gave me a funny look so I quickly added, "Of course, I try not to play into all that noise, and people don't know what he's really like behind closed doors and all…"

"It's probably jealousy," she said. "You know there have been a number of women who've tried to win his heart, but all they got was a wild ride." She grinned and chuckled. "I'm not saying you won't have a challenge, but you're a stronger woman than he's used to. All those groupies will pale when he accepts that a strong woman can like him, that he doesn't have to settle for the easy ones, the ones who fall all over themselves to get him into bed."

I laughed. "What makes you such an expert on guys like Blake?" I felt slightly uncomfortable having this type of conversation with the team owner's eighteen-year-old daughter. I hoped I wasn't being set up in a trap.

She tipped her head. "Do you really want to know?"

Suddenly, I did. "Yes."

"I had a crush on a player a few years ago. When Daddy found out…well, let's just say that he hated the idea and ultimately it didn't work out."

"You broke it off?"

She scowled. "He left. Moved on."

"Sorry." Clearly Daphne had her heart broken at a young age and I hurt for her.

"One good thing that came from it was that mom and I had a long talk about guys like that—like Blake Collins. She pointed out that it made sense to fall for them—the ones that are such hunks. I mean some of them are so hot; some are even charming off the ice. She said that the problem is that so often they get so much attention, get so full of themselves that they act out with women. They think you'll love them no matter what sort of shit they pull."

I thought her mom made a great point. "So, she warned you off them?"

Daphne grinned. "Actually, no. She said that those guys had a lot to recommend them. That for some women, a macho guy, a real alpha type made life good. But…"

"But what?"

"Well, she gave me this strange smile and told me that Blake Collins reminds her a lot of Daddy—how he was before they got married. He was a hot shot player too, and she said he was as wild as they came."

"That's hard to imagine. He's so... I don't know... dignified."

"She said that's the result of good training." She winked. This conversation was getting stranger and stranger.

"Training."

"She said you need to have the guts to stand toe-to-toe with a monster like that and set down the rules."

"The rules?" I wanted to laugh. I was also a little shocked that Daphne's mom used the word "monster" to refer to her own husband.

"Mom said if a guy like that turns you on, the last thing you want is to change him. The thing is to let them know what you expect and see if they're willing to play by your rules, just like they have to on the ice. And when they don't..." she grinned, "...you need to resort to the penalty box."

"And that works?"

"According to Mom it does. Daddy remains a bad boy in the ways she likes." I found that hard to believe, but only nodded along in agreement.

"I see. And do you have your eye on a hockey player now?"

She smiled wistfully. "Not now. I decided to play things slow."

"You have time." She was still a baby in my opinion. When I was eighteen, I hadn't even been in a serious relationship yet.

"Speaking of time—it's time to drop the puck." She pointed to the screen. "The opening face-off. Blake will be lined up on the center's left shoulder where he can get a good line on the puck."

We watched the two teams line up behind their centers, each man tense, ready. The puck dropped, sticks clashed, the puck shot out toward Blake who flicked it to a teammate and the game was on.

"You can breathe again," Daphne laughed. "Sit back and enjoy whatever happens."

11

BLAKE

It was crappy anytime you lost a game, but when the team was in the playoffs, every game was critical. "What the fuck was wrong with you out there Collins?" the coach bellowed as we went into the locker room.

I didn't have an answer. "I couldn't get the pace." I hadn't played badly. I'd made no mistakes, but I hadn't played well either. I felt like I'd let my team down.

"You treated them like visiting royalty. You get paid to kick their asses, not to let them do what they want. They walked all over you."

"It won't happen again." I looked him in the eye. I meant it. I'd probably spend half of the next game in the penalty box, but they'd be bleeding.

The coach glared at me with a look of fire and brimstone, looking to see if I meant it. "If it does, I'll find someone who wants to play hockey, not go ice skating." My heart flipped, and then I felt a surge of humiliation.

When the coach stormed off, probably to get his ass

chewed out in turn by Tom Lassiter, Randall came over and slapped me on the shoulder. "It happens," he said. "A little fresh pussy fogs the brain. If you've decided to marry this one, she must be special enough to keep you busy every night."

I shook my head, not really knowing how to respond to that.

Fresh pussy? Truth was, Chloe was messing me up on multiple levels that had nothing to do with my dick. Randall had seen us at the restaurant and jumped to the conclusion I was screwing her. It was logical. He'd teased me about that at practice. Now that we'd announced the engagement, he was a happy boy. More groupies might steer his way if I was "taken."

When I came out of the locker room, I found Chloe waiting. She was a sight for sore eyes the way her wavy blond hair fell over her shoulders.

I opened my arms and she slipped into them, molding in a perfect fit, and I realized how great it was to have her there, waiting for me. Her hair smelled like coconuts and it drew me in even more. As my teammates came out, passing us, some laughing, I kissed her. I didn't even care what they thought about me in that moment. My eyes were clouded by Chloe, her perfect feminine scent and beautiful curves. Those warm, soft, lips touched mine, sending a tingle through me that was sexually potent, yet more than that. There was some sort of connection I felt to her that went above lust and wanting to fuck her. Happiness filled me when she was around.

Around Chloe I was beginning to realize I'd never had a real relationship with a woman before, I didn't even know what it had felt like. Not a complete relationship. I wasn't sure I'd known it was possible. There were women you knew and did business with, even chatted with, and then there were the ones you fucked. I couldn't anticipate a feeling that I'd like to have a relationship where there was sex but also talking and friendship added in the mix. I'd thought I'd cross the line with Chloe, get a woman I did business with to spread her legs for me. Instead of that, the boundaries were blurring. I wanted her, but I also wanted to be with her and wanted her to care for me, the way she pretended to. I didn't want it to be just for the cameras anymore, I wanted her for real.

It was unsettling. It was intoxicating.

"Come with me," she said, her voice sensual and sweet, like honey.

She led me out into the parking garage. The usual crowd of women were there, clinging to my teammates. One saw us and shouted, "You don't deserve him, bitch!" Chloe winced but said nothing. I admired her dignified form against the crazy die-hards. We pushed through the crowd as a limo pulled up. The driver hopped out and opened the door for us. I felt a new rush of sexual energy as I studied her bare legs. Her skirt hiked up as she sat down, making my fingers tremble to touch.

I realized the ache inside me was longing.

The driver shut the door and Chloe turned and kissed me. Women beat on the windows, furious. "They don't want you taken out of circulation," she said.

Hearing her words, watching those lovely lips saying them, I began to think that I might like being taken out of circulation—by this woman. I didn't know, of course, but I had an idea that she could keep me satisfied, interested, like no other woman I'd ever known. This was the longest I'd ever held attention on a woman in my entire life, but I wasn't bored yet.

Her phone rang and she answered. She pushed a button. "Blake and I are in a limo, Ralph. I'm putting you on speaker."

"It looks as if the plan is going in the right direction," he said. "This morning I got a call from an agency that handles endorsements...the one I've been talking to, and they have some interested companies. He doesn't want to rush things because bigger fish will probably be interested as well. And, of course, Blake, that assumes you get your head out of your ass and play hockey."

"Yeah," I said. "I already got that tender ass reaming by the coach." I rolled my eyes.

"Keep in mind that any endorsement deal is going to be contingent on you getting your contract renewed, and from the way Tom Lassiter screamed in my ear, he isn't thinking kindly of you at the moment."

I felt the need to defend myself. I played great all the time. I had one bad day and I felt like I was thrown to the sharks. "Everyone has a day when..."

"Starting players don't, my friend—not during the playoffs."

"I'll be on it tomorrow," I promised, and I meant it.

"Good. Keep in mind that if you're the driving force throughout the playoffs, that new contract will include a more than healthy payday. You just have to play this game for a little while and then you can go back to being the asshole only you know how to be. Do this for yourself, do it for me."

"I'll be on my game."

Chloe put it in her pocket. I looked over at her. She seemed distant. She was like a light switch that turned on and off. The car had pulled away and the crowds were long gone. With them, the cameras, the reporters, the fans. I was afraid my fake life was becoming more important to me than my real life—and that was going to end in nothing but complete fucking disaster.

Fake Fiancé

"What is it?" I asked her, but she simply turned her face away and stared out the window. I sat back, feeling the frosty silence and wondering what had her so deeply upset.

"I'll play well next week," I said again, feeling sick. It was like talking to an empty room.

12

BLAKE

Her limo took us back to my place. The entire way I noted a swarm of cars around us.

"I wonder why there's so much traffic?"

"Reporters," she said curtly. "They're going to be after blood now."

"Why? Has something changed?" I felt some nervous jitters start to rise from within me. I hated being kept in the dark about things.

"I'll tell you inside."

I unlocked the door and when we went in she closed the blinds, frustrating the reporters who'd managed to find places that gave them a view. "What the hell is wrong with you?" she asked. I could hear the muffled sound of reporters talking outside.

I looked at her, studying that face of hers splayed in anger and I had no idea where it was coming from. "Wrong with me? What the fuck are you talking about?"

"The reason there are more reporters out there than ever is that they're looking for the reason Blake Collins suddenly is off his game." She threw her hands up in exasperation. "You're a god on the ice, Blake. What is going on with you?"

I shrugged. I had no idea, but I was pretty sure I was staring at it. For the first time in my life, I wanted something else more than I wanted to play hockey.

"Ralph was right. Tom was furious. The way you played was not what the crowd or the team wanted to see. Your heart wasn't in it."

He shrugged. "I played okay, it wasn't perfect but it wasn't total shit either." I didn't care for the way she was chastising me. She had no idea what it was like out there.

"It's just not you, Blake." Was that a compliment? From the ice queen? The woman who could barely stand to look at me? That got my attention. "The trouble is that you should've won that game."

As much as I hated this moment where she was talking to me like a child, I knew she was right and that stung. Winnipeg hadn't played their best game and we had several chances to win it, but we blew it instead. I blew it. "Don't worry. I'll get it back."

"You better. You're already fighting an uphill battle to get your contract renewed. And the endorsements depend on you playing a top game. There is no point in cleaning up your image if your game goes into the toilet. I'm trying to *help* you here Blake, but you have to meet me halfway."

I sat down on the couch, watching her, taking in her posture. She was upset, but I didn't think it was about the hockey game. Not all of it at least. I didn't know if I had let her down too. I didn't want her to be disappointed in me. Why I cared about her opinion, I had no idea, but I did. A lot.

"Yeah, well no one can be one-hundred percent all the time." I still felt the need to defend myself a little. I wasn't the only damn player on the team after all. I couldn't carry everybody. It wasn't my job to babysit my teammates.

She gave me a thin smile. "They are going to think that you lost your edge. That being in love changed you."

"So now I'm in love and I've lost my edge?" I scoffed.

"That's what they'll think."

"I feel like I have to be two people. That's fucking hard." I wanted to say that she had no idea because she was seemingly emotionless but I bit my tongue.

"Two people?"

"I was this bad boy who kicks ass on the ice and now I'm supposed to be this regular guy with a fiancée? What's next, two kids and a dog? I'm trying to get into that, but it fucks with my head. I can't just switch back and forth. Cut me some fucking slack." I blew out a frustrated puff of air.

"You're complicating things, Blake."

"How's that?"

"No one wants to lose the bad boy."

"Then what? You guys told me I have to behave, rein it in or lose everything. Now I'm in deep shit for doing that."

"The bad boy needs to stay. All they want you to change is that you aren't seen as whoring around."

"Isn't that what bad boys do? How am I supposed to still play the part of bad boy? Nobody is going to believe a woman would stick around for that kind of guy."

She took a breath. "What we're selling is the idea that you've found one girl, one who won't put up with that, you've focused on her."

I grinned at her. I thought I was finally getting what she was saying. "So, it would be okay if I went out front and beat the shit out of one of the reporters?"

"Absolutely. If you made it seem that you were pissed about them cutting in on your private time."

I gave her a meaningful look. I didn't like the way things were going any more than she did. I hadn't been able to get

Fake Fiancé

my head in the game and that sucked. I needed some clarification. It was time to put some cards on the table. "And what about you?"

"What about me?"

"If I'm supposed to still be a bad, if controlled boy, why are you testing me?"

"Testing you how?"

"To see if I'd jump through your hoops. You've loved sending the message that I'd better behave—your words."

She looked alarmed. "Sure. It's been about your public image."

"Then why these games in private?" I was trying to bait her into admitting her own flaws.

She looked surprised. "Blake, everything I've done is to get your contract renewed and help you get the endorsements. I'm trying to earn my paycheck," she said flatly as if I meant nothing to her other than dollar signs.

"Bullshit. You're flaunting your body, or cuddling up to me and taking things up to the point where I'd…you've been trying to make me lose control so you could tell the bosses I couldn't play your game."

She swallowed. "Not at all. They don't care how you act in private."

I could see I'd rattled her, which gave me back some power over the situation and I took advantage. "Then explain all this shit where you pretend you're attracted to me, that you want me. Or are you going to pretend my fake fiancée likes bad boys too?"

"What? That had nothing to do with… Blake, do you really think that was some kind of damn test?"

I smiled. "Finally, she gets it. That's exactly what I think—you decided to make me pay for roping you into playing this role. You decided to punish me by trying to make me crazy with the way you've been acting. Then you get what you want, but if I do…watch out. There goes the deal." She lost her poker face after that. I had won this one, but somehow still felt like shit.

13

CHLOE

I looked up at Blake in absolute disbelief and dismay. How could the man not know how I felt about him? Was he really so blind that when I threw myself at him he thought I was testing him? "You are an absolute idiot, Blake Collins!" I spat out in utter frustration at his lack of mental perception.

"Then explain." His eyes blazed.

"You think that the other night was all about your career?"

"What else?" He shrugged.

I pushed him backward, up against the wall, watching his eyes dilate as I pulled his face down and kissed him hard. His cologne smelled amazing. His lips were soft and edible. "I want you, you stupid bastard. I was coming on to you and you...you stopped too soon."

He hesitated for the blink of an eye—a blink that seemed an eternity while I waited for him to say something or at least move. I held my breath, and then he grabbed me. "You are so fucking hot," he said, and then he kissed me back, with more passion and desperation than before. It was a rough, passionate kiss that sent a shockwave rippling through me and I found it exhilarating.

I'd wanted an animal and it seemed I'd unleashed one because he was tearing at my dress. Buttons went flying and his hands were scalding hot on my breasts. He bent his face down and sucked a nipple into his mouth and a moan of pleasure escaped my lips. He hiked my dress up my hips and he was tugging at my panties, pulling them down to my knees. I let them fall to my ankles and then I stepped out of them.

He undid his pants and brought out his hard cock. I gasped at the glorious sight of it. It was rigid and I felt the heat of it radiate on my bare thigh. He kept himself pressed against me, teasing me into oblivion. He pulled a condom from his pocket and opened it with his teeth, his eyes wild and sparkling. Then he put the condom on. My eyes were glued to that massive, throbbing shaft of his and I wanted him more than ever.

Suddenly, he scooped my legs up. I squealed playfully. My heels came off as he tucked my legs over his powerful arms, pushing my back against the wall. My breathing kept pace with my heart, rapid and desperate. He kissed me again and I felt his sheathed cock at my pussy lips, giving me a surge and tingle of pleasure. He fumbled for a second, working it inside me with his right hand, then he grunted and drove it into me with full amazing force. I cried out with the thrill and sensation of his rock hard cock finally inside of me. "Oh fuck!" I shouted.

He slammed into me, standing me up against that goddamn wall, taking me with his hard length. I couldn't believe how full it made me feel. His hands were against the wall as he thrust in and out of me.

"God, what an awesome, gorgeously tight pussy," he

moaned in my ear as he buried himself in me and showered my neck with whispered kisses.

I hooked my heels behind him and dug them into his hips. I had my fingers interlocked behind his neck as my bad boy took me, half clothed in his living room and I loved it. He grabbed my hair and pulled it, making me cry out in ecstasy again. I loved the blend of pleasure and pain.

Having Blake fuck me was better than I'd imagined. It was incredible; it was everything I had been missing. His hot cock moving in me was magical and suddenly I was losing control, I was dangling on the precipice of orgasm. And then, just at that moment, he kissed me again, put his mouth over mine and forced his tongue in my mouth to possess it at the same time that his cock owned my pussy.

My body convulsed with a massive fit of pleasure.

"Holy shit," he moaned and I knew the contractions of my muscles were caressing his cock and he would soon go over the edge too. His breath grew ragged, his face was a sheen of sweat, and I swooned as his cock pulsed inside me as he came.

When he finished, we clung to each other for a time, taking heaving breaths as we came down from climax. I was afraid to move, to shatter the moment. And then, finally, he slipped out of me, and I put my feet on the floor.

He stared at me in a combination of sated pleasure and disbelief. I knew the look. It was exactly how I felt.

14

BLAKE

I couldn't believe what had happened; it seemed as if the world was spinning fast and in slow motion at the same time. Everything had gotten swept up in a mad swirl of passion and insane emotions that we finally caved in and let consume us. She'd finally asked me to fuck her. It was what I'd wanted. Well, not exactly. She hadn't begged for me to take her, she'd demanded it. Although she made it clear she wanted me to fuck her it sure as hell hadn't been submissive.

Still, it was intense and carnal and I wanted more. I wanted her.

She stripped off her dress, letting it fall to the floor, showing me that luscious body. I couldn't remember seeing a sexier woman. She wasn't shy or coy. She looked right at me with those piercing eyes of hers that drove me crazy, letting me know that she wanted more too. But I couldn't shake the idea that it was also a challenge, that she wanted me to know that I couldn't resist her and she had the upper hand.

I had no interest in resisting her. After fucking her against the wall, there was no point to it. I was still

Fake Fiancé

suspicious of her motives and wanted to stay on my A game. It was hard to believe she only wanted a hard fuck, but if she thought that my desire was a weakness, if she thought the sight of her body made me so crazy that she was in control, I was going to have to show her just how wrong she was. I'd wanted her, and I still wanted her, but not on her terms. I was going to take her and screw her senseless. She'd made it clear I could have her and I intended to fuck her until she knew who was in charge, who held the upper hand in the desire game.

I took a breath to clear my head. This was my territory now, home ice. I watched her walk to the wet bar and pour herself a drink, then turned and faced me again, sipping it while still unclothed, naked and raw. I took her in, let my gaze roam over those firm breasts and delicious curves. She was intoxicating and luring me in again. She was daring me, waiting to see if I'd make my move.

I undid my shirt, tossing it on the couch. Her eyes never wavered. Her teasing had done its work and I was already hard again—it jutted out defiantly and her eyes went to it and stayed on it as I kicked off my shoes, then pulled off my socks and pants. I stood before her, naked and aroused, dick pointing to the sky. She sipped her drink as I walked toward her. "I'll have some of that," I said.

She nodded and winked at me. She turned away, and picked up a glass to pour me a drink.

"Not that," I told her. My voice was husky with desire. The way the sight of her lithe, naked body aroused me was surprising and wonderful. Her perky tits made my mouth water, her perfect skin made me want to run my hands all over her.

A quizzical look came over her face. "Vodka then?"

I put my hand on her bare ass and squeezed, and felt her stiffen. "No. I want some more of this." I nuzzled her neck and saw her swallow. That excited me even more, seeing her uncertainty. Just that fast I was back in control of the situation. If she was wondering what sort of passion she'd unleashed, she was about to find out.

I stepped behind her and reached around to grab her soft, firm breasts. I pulled her back against my chest and my cock brushed her ass and along her thigh. A sigh escaped her lips and she set her glass on the table; her hands came up to my face and stroked my cheek.

Despite her earlier demand for me to fuck her, despite the strip tease she'd done, I half expected her to protest. Taking her when she'd crossed the line and then tried to control me would be almost as good as having her beg me to fuck her again.

But there was no protests. To my surprise, she rubbed her round ass against me and practically purred. Even when I moved my hands down her body, over her belly, over the bare nether lips, crooking one finger to part them and run between them, she only moaned softly and writhed erotically against me. My dick was pulsing with longing to be back inside her tight wet and warm core. The moist heat of her pussy welcomed my finger, and I wiggled it around inside, tickling her clit.

"I'm going to fuck you, Chloe," I told her. "Again."

"Yes," she said, her voice soft and I heard a hint of pleading there.

"I'm going to fuck you until you can't move. I'm going to get so deep inside you that you'll never get me out." I grabbed another condom packet and tore it open, then put the condom in her hand. "Put that on me," I smiled, charmed to order her around. She tensed again. "I want you to kneel down and put that on my cock."

She closed her hand over it, then turned and faced me, hesitating a beat before she dropped to her knees and I felt the delicious touch of her fingers on me and she unrolled it over my swollen shaft. She stared up at me, questioningly and I took her arms and pulled her to her feet and scooped her into my arms. She was light and delicate; her hand ran over my chest, a caress as I carried her into my bedroom and put her on the bed. There was desire in her eyes as she looked up at me and I crawled up on the bed, hooking one of her legs over my shoulder.

"I'm going to take you slowly," I told her. I wanted to start off slow and gentle this time. I craved her body, wanted this to last an eternity. Her lips parted and her tongue flicked over them. "Open up for me," I said. "Spread that pussy open with your fingers."

Her pupils dilated and her hand slowly moved down to do as I'd told her, splaying the lips apart and showing me the pink flesh of her pussy.

I wanted nothing more than to slam into her, bury my throbbing prick in her and take her hard, but this was going to be special—a slow, mind-blowing fuck. I was going to shut the whole world out until it was just the two of us. Watching my cock move between her slender fingers and into that sweet, wet pussy made my heart pound. The enveloping warmth caressed me and she arched her back as I took her in one, sweet, slow thrust that didn't stop until my body pressed against that upturned thigh. Her mouth was open as I reversed the process, withdrawing slowly. My cock urged me to thrust with purpose, for a quick climax, but I wanted to make it last as long as I could.

She squirmed magnificently as I continued slow fucking her.

"Fuck me hard," she said, but I kept on grinding my hips on her excruciatingly slow. In this position I could watch my cock possess her, fill that lovely pussy. I could feel her muscles as she tried to work them, to excite me enough that

I'd lose control. After a time I heard the sound of her breathing growing ragged and I knew she was close to coming. That would be perfect, feeling her riding her orgasm.

She gasped, closed her eyes and shuddered, once again arching her back. This was better than I'd imagined it could be. Her face was contorted with the pleasure and she bucked her hips, wanting more of my cock inside her. My hand drifted down to her pussy and rubbed over her clit and she moaned. When her eyes fluttered open I pulled out of her, shifting to move between those legs, lifting them, holding the back by resting them on my chest and moving my body over hers. I got my cock back between her pussy lips and impaled her with it, driving it balls deep. I began fucking her in a frenzy. Her nails dug into my arms and she was moaning "yes," over and over as I thrust as hard as I could. Her tits bounced up and down with the movement.

Soon, too soon, I exploded, shooting my cum inside her.

When I rolled off her, she wiped my sweaty face with her hand, then kissed me. I lay there, exhausted and sated for the moment.

We lay together in a heap of collapsed passion, my body feeling like jelly from the two orgasms. She rubbed my back, her fingertips grazing over my skin. It sent a surge of chill bumps all over me. I loved our bodies intertwined. After a time, my eyelids became so heavy that I gave into a welcomed sleep. I woke feeling sweat drying on my body and cum drying on my thigh. Chloe slept on her side and I watched her in the shadowy room. There was enough light that I could make out her outline and feel the heat of her body. It was almost as if I needed to fuck her again just so I could believe that it was real, that we had done it before and it wasn't a dream.

Her breathing was almost imperceptible but touching

her, setting my hand on the delicious mound of her breast made her gasp. Her hand moved toward me, touched my cock and then her fingers ensnared it. "It's so soft and growing stiff," she whispered. It sounded so erotic in that dark, in my bed. She stroked it gently. When it was erect, she reached to the nightstand for a condom and put it on me. I trembled at her delicate touch, the way it felt as she rolled it on. Then she bent her face down to kiss it before stretching out again.

"Please fuck me again," she said. I couldn't see her face in the dark but I could feel her longing.

Her voice was soft and hushed. She had said exactly the words I'd been wanting to hear, but what she communicated was somehow different. She was begging for it, begging for me to fuck her, but there was no surrender in her voice.

And now I didn't need her to surrender. I only needed her to keep wanting more, keep wanting me.

I ran my hand down from her breast, over the soft curve of her belly. She took my wrist and moved my hand to her pussy. My fingers played in the moist warmth, then I rolled her onto her side, facing away from me. I moved up close and she lifted her leg to let my throbbing cock slide over her swollen lips from behind. I tucked her foot behind my leg. My lips tasted the back of her neck and my hand caressed a breast.

"Put it in," I said, then held my breath as her fingertips touched the head of my cock and pressed it up between her nether lips. I pulled my hips back slightly and when I felt the warmth of her tender flesh, I pushed them forward again, savoring the sigh that escaped her lips as my cock entered her.

We rocked together and the muscles inside her worked their magic on me. I slid my hand down to touch her pussy, to rub it as I thrust into her and was rewarded by her breathing growing ragged. I wasn't sure how long I could last with us taking each other to the edge this way.

"Come for me," she whispered. "I want you to come."

Her words took me that final distance and I cried out as I spent, shooting my semen into the condom inside her.

I might have fallen asleep after that, everything was hazy. I'd gotten what I thought I wanted. I was satisfied sexually but now the goals had changed. I just wanted her, and I didn't even care what else happened.

That kind of thinking was dangerous. But lying next to her in bed, everything else faded to black in the back of my mind, the playoffs, the sponsorship deals, the fans, the parties…all of it. There was only Chloe, her soft skin pressed to mine, the way she smelled, the soft sounds she made as she snuggled closer—like I wasn't an undeserving asshole. For the first time in years, the buzzing in my chest, the echoing emptiness that drove me, was full. Of her.

"You're going to ruin me," I whispered against ear.

She murmured something and pulled my arm more tightly to her chest, like I was her personal blanket. I knew she was asleep and that somehow made the unconscious act all the more endearing. I'd have to tell her the truth soon. I needed her to know that I was tired of playing this game, that long after the contracts were signed I wanted to keep that ring on her finger. We would set a date and get married for real. That was what I wanted—her, my Chloe.

I slept for a time and then woke to her kissing my cheek. She was dressed. "I'm leaving now. You need to get ready for the game. I'll see you afterward. Kick ass out there, bad boy."

I wanted to tell her to stay, to get back in my bed, that I wasn't ready to part with her yet, but she was back on the script—it was as if we hadn't fucked our brains out in a wonderful passionate night.

Later I'd explain it all to her, tell her how much she meant to me. I'd explain how things would be different from now on.

But for now, she was right. I had to sleep. I had to be ready for the game. I needed to get my shit together and kick some ass.

15

CHLOE

It had been a mistake, a huge, probably colossal mistake to have sex with Blake Collins. Let alone have sex with him *three fucking times.* When I'd left, he gave me a smile. It was a satisfied, pleased with himself smile that made me think that I'd screwed up and now he'd won or something. I shook my head and looked to the ceiling in frustration.

I'd let him have me and that was what he'd been after from the beginning. That was why he'd asked me to play the fiancée. He'd intended to get me into bed, to show me that I couldn't resist him. I was a fucking idiot for falling for his tricks. I was not a fan of self-loathing, but I sure was going to mentally kick my own ass after this.

That he'd been right from the very beginning made it hurt more. Now that I'd done what he wanted, let him have me, and worse, let him see how much I'd wanted it, it was over. He might play along publicly, but privately he'd be wanting me to acknowledge that the bad boy could get any woman he wanted, including me.

And I couldn't avoid him. Now I had to be more on in

Fake Fiancé

front of the cameras than ever, even though I wanted to crawl into a hole and give up instead. Game two of the playoffs was coming up and I had a part to play—the loyal fiancée cheering her hero to victory.

I went home and got out my laptop to do some work, focusing on trivial things that would take my mind off the fact that sex with Blake had been incredible. I had undeniably enjoyed every second of it. I'd never come so powerfully—I'd never come twice with a man in one night. My mind kept going back to those memories. My brain would flash back to his naked body on top of me, sweaty and hard. And it was more than simple sex. Being with him made me feel better than I'd ever felt, I had sexual confidence I never knew existed. Knowing he'd wanted me had been a thrill. I turned on the hockey star, the sexy bad boy and I was proud of that fact. Now he'd had his way with me. I was trapped by my own desire because I *wanted* him to use my body as his sex toy. If I let him fuck me again, he'd think he owned me; if I didn't, he could laugh because he'd already gotten what he wanted and that thought made me cringe.

When the phone rang, I was happy for the distraction. It was Ralph Dodge.

"Your plan is working," he said. "Of course, he's got to get his game back on track, but the endorsements are pretty much in place if we renew his contract."

I sighed with relief. "Wonderful. How is that part going?"

"I talked with Tom and he's happy about the image. If Blake brings his game back up to snuff today we can be sure he'll renew. The better he plays, the better the offer Tom will make. As long as the game goes well today, he wants to renew it right away. In that case we can call off the PR game early."

I knew that would be a relief for Ralph. Getting those contracts was the point of the exercise, after all. I knew I should be happy...delighted even. My plan was working, everything as I'd intended. I'd kept Blake in line and the offers would soon be on the table. He could sign the contracts, then we'd split up. "That's great, Ralph. Let me tell Blake—after the game."

"Good idea," he said.

The idea made my stomach tighten painfully. I didn't want it to be over. I wanted...I wanted Blake to love me. It was ending before it even got started it seemed, and I detested the thought of saying goodbye to him.

I wanted this bad boy to love me. What kind of a fool would hope that a playboy like that would settle for one woman? He never had shown interest before in settling down, so what made me any different? Nothing, I was certain of it. I wasn't interested in sharing him with other women. I was greedy, hungry and starving for him. I wanted him. He'd fucked me, but I wouldn't settle for that. It wasn't enough. I needed a deeper, more profound relationship with him. I wanted to be his best friend. I wanted to go to the movies or to restaurants together when it wasn't an act and we could joke and laugh and go home to make love freely at the end of the night.

I'd have to do something dramatic when this was over. I'd have to make some kind of change, but I had no idea what. I needed some sort of distractive hobby to help me forget.

Blake Collins had gotten inside me both physically and mentally and I'd need time to sort out what I wanted life to be like after him. The void would be huge but I knew time would close and heal it. Frank wouldn't dare object to me taking a month off after a major coup like this, so at least I had that to look forward to. I could go somewhere nice...one of those resorts that took care of everything and you concentrated on your tan while hot bartenders served up margaritas. I might even meet some guy who wasn't a jock, who wasn't deliberate trouble and let him sweep me off my feet, take me to bed and…

The trouble was, I didn't want any of that. I didn't want the time with Blake to end. I didn't want to rebound with a sexy bartender on a white sandy beach. Looking at the engagement ring on my finger made my stomach knot up again. As if to mirror my feelings, the ring dazzled and sparkled as bright as I'd ever seen it, with amazing color hues. What I wanted was for the engagement to be real, and to keep the ring on my finger forever. I wanted it to be meaningful and I wanted Blake to look at me and see me with the same pair of eyes as I now viewed him.

Don't be an idiot! I shook my head again trying to skip back to reality. Blake Collins didn't want someone like me except for a night in his bed, using me for his pleasure. I told myself this while I looked at my reflection, sad eyes in the mirror. The only problem was, I didn't want to believe a word of it.

16

BLAKE

It was a glorious day and I felt on top of the world. From the moment I walked out of the house to get in the cab, I knew things had changed. And the instant I hit the ice I knew that I was going to own the game. I had no idea how I knew that before they even dropped the puck, but I did. It was like everything was right...all the stars lined up exactly right, or some shit. The sun was shining, the birds were chirping. It was time to cue all those clichés when it came to feeling good.

I had the burn that day and was ready to go into beast mode. Winnipeg sensed it and it threw them off their game. Fear was in their eyes as I barreled towards them shaving ice along the way. I felt like I was playing a team from the minors—I could read their body language and when I couldn't I damn well made them read mine, checking guys into the boards so that they thought twice about messing with me. I allowed my love of the game to take control of my mind and body.

It was a slaughter and tied the playoffs up. I knew I could

keep going too. And I knew why. Her name was Chloe, and she was the new fuel to my fire.

I'd been angry, upset that she left in the morning the way she had. I'd wanted to spend the day in bed with her, getting up for breakfast and then right back to burying myself in her. I'd wanted to be wrapped up in her. I'd felt like a spoiled child who wasn't getting their way when she left and I didn't want her to, but I knew I had to snap right out of that shit.

She was right and I knew it. There was a game to play, and my focus had to be on that. It was the playoffs and Chloe had told me to kick ass, so that's what I was going to do. I always wanted to kick ass, but today I felt like I had the world with me and I was going to push the envelope.

Chloe was standing outside the locker room, in the security area, looking nervous.

"What's the matter?" I asked.

"It's over," she said, her eyes soft and sad on the inside, but the tough shell exterior was trying to hold on.

"What do you mean?" I gave her a half hug in greeting.

"You played the best game of your life. Tom is sending a contract offer to Ralph tomorrow. The endorsements are pretty much a slap shot away too." She twisted the ring on her finger. "So, the game, the one we've been playing is almost over. A few days and I can give this back. You've gotten everything you wanted. Congratulations." She said the last part flatly and it sent a dagger through my heart.

"Oh, sure," I said curtly. I looked at her face and began to understand. "You think last night was just about getting you, having sex with you?" I leaned in until our faces were only an inch or two apart. I could feel her breath.

"What else?" She shrugged nonchalantly.

I sighed. "I do want that ring back."

"Of course. As soon as things are signed. Then we can announce the wedding is off."

"No."

She started. "Of course. You'll want to go back to your life."

"You can't ever wind things back to some previous time, Chloe. Your plan, this game we played changed too many things." I gave her a deep and profound stare.

"I don't understand." She looked at me in confusion. I couldn't believe she *still* didn't understand what I was trying to say to her.

"With what's happened, I see life differently now that you've entered it. I didn't play better just because I felt good. Today I feel different about life on a new level. It didn't just happen this morning of course, but it took me a while to see what was going on."

"And what was that?" She crossed her arms. She was being stubborn but I was determined to get through to her.

"That I was falling in love with you. I learned that my desire for you, to be with you, is insatiable." I pushed a strand of hair off her face affectionately.

"But…" She tried to protest once more, so I pressed on.

"I do want that ring back, but only because it's part of this crappy charade we played. I want to get rid of it." I reached in my pocket and held out a box. "I got this out of my safe this morning. It isn't stylish, like that one, but it was my grandmother's." I held it out to her.

She opened the box and her mouth opened, her eyes flashed in wonderment. "It's gorgeous."

"We can return the other one, or sell it."

She blinked. "You want me to have this ring?"

"Well, what I want is for you to agree to marry me. For real." At that statement I got down on one bended knee, for a true proposal to the woman I now loved unconditionally.

She stood stock still, staring at me. I wondered if my

heart had stopped or if it was just that the world had frozen solid.

17

CHLOE

I was certain I had to look like a complete fool, standing there staring at Blake the way I was. I gaped at the ring in amazement, unsure how to react. All I could do was stare at the ring, words caught in my throat. I couldn't look him in the eye because I knew I would cry.

"I want you to marry me," he said again. He was trying to convince me of something I knew I already felt deep down. His grin had an amazing boyish quality about it, excited and hopeful.

"I have to think," I said and shook my head, and his grin faded, collapsed and vanished. But it was true. I could barely breathe, much less think. I couldn't say yes on a whim like this, no matter what my heart was trying to sing to me.

"Sure," he said. He took the tiny black box with the ring in it and shoved it in his pocket. I saw the hurt in his eyes. He expected me to immediately explode with joyous enthusiasm, but so much about him overwhelmed me that even though he was asking the question I hadn't dared hope he would ask, even though I knew it was exactly what I wanted, I needed a clear head—to be certain. I needed time to really know if he was serious about this.

"Take your time," he said. He gave me a chagrined half crushed smile.

I turned away from him, clutching that box, the wonderful ring, dazzling and beautiful. It was also heartfelt because it had belonged to his grandmother. That meant it had depth and meaning. He had deemed me worthy enough to wear it and picked me against all the odds. I knew what to do. It was in everyone's interest for me to just walk away, take the time to think this through. I wanted it, but that was my body talking, not my head. We were nothing alike, he was night and I was day. We came from such different backgrounds, a marriage like that…how would it survive?

I thought back to my earlier conversation with Tom Lassiter's daughter, Daphne. How she had told me his wife had basically "trained" him on how to behave. Did I want to be that nagging wife? Did I want to change who a person was?

Walking away from him, having that uncertainty hanging there, was painful. And dammit, I'd lived my life listening to my head. It had gotten me success in business and an empty personal life. What kind of idiot gambled in business and played it safe in love? The universe would find a way for us.

I turned back and saw him standing there, my stoic warrior, and realized I wouldn't be asking him to change. He was a man who made his own choices and I loved his confidence, his arrogant alpha male attitude. I loved the way he wasn't shy about what he wanted.

The question was not would I change Blake. The real question was, would he change me? And the answer was no. I was every bit as stubborn as he was. If he was in my world, and my bed, would be play by my rules?

He'd have to.

Did he know that?

"Blake..." I said.

He looked at me levelly, showing nothing, but I knew the answer. Yes, he knew the rules of this game, he knew and he still wanted to play. There was heat in his eyes, and hunger, and something vulnerable I'd never seen before. It was his pain that broke me. He was offering me everything, expecting to be hurt. "What, baby?"

"I thought about it, and...the answer is yes."

A light flickered in his eyes, a tiny smile twitched in his lips. "You'll marry me?"

"Yes." I grinned at him and edged ever closer until we were almost touching. My heart was beating out of my chest.

"Good, because without that this engagement shit sucks." I laughed at our little joke. He came over and stood behind me, wrapping those strong arms around me and pulling me against his hard body. I felt the tremors of arousal coursing through me.

"When the season is over, when you've kicked Winnipeg asses across the ice, we can announce our wedding date at the ceremony, after you get the trophy." I gazed up at him, happy to plan our future together.

He nuzzled my neck. "We can honeymoon in Tahiti. I read about a place with huts on private beaches, on a private island. And no ice."

"Yes, that sounds delicious," I practically cooed as I stood there in his embrace, and his hands, touching my thighs and moving up under my skirt to stroke me through my silk panties felt even more delicious. "I've dreamed about just such a resort, with a thatched roof cottage on the beach. We can have a big wedding here, then slip away to that private island, where we can walk naked."

"Walk?" His fingers slipped under the crotch of my panties and into my wet pussy. "I intend to have my way with

Fake Fiancé

you, Chloe. I'm going to fuck this sweet pussy so much that you won't be able to do much walking." He moved his hips rubbing his crotch against my ass, letting me feel his growing erection.

"That sounds wonderful," I said, trying to breathe through the pleasure.

"I guess that means we have a lot to do. I need to win this playoff and the easiest way to do that is to win the next three games in row, then we have to arrange for the wedding and the reception…"

I wiggled my hips and felt his cock hard against my ass. "You win the playoffs and I'll take care of those details."

"A fair division of labor. I assume I'll get my assignments."

I laughed. "Your first assignment as my husband is going to be getting me pregnant." I wanted a baby desperately.

He turned me around and kissed me hard, pressing me back against the wall. Grabbing my blouse he pulled the elastic of the neck and tugged it down my shoulders, baring my breasts and putting his mouth on my nipple, sucking it hard. He hiked my skirt up to my waist and put his hand between my legs, pulling the crotch of my panties to one side and running a finger inside me. I moaned. "What are you doing?" We were still in a semi-public area.

With his body pinning me against the wall, he unzipped his pants and took out his swollen cock. It had never looked so big, or so beautiful and I loved how it was all mine for the rest of my life. "Getting you pregnant is a big and important job."

I reached for him hungrily and wrapped my fingers around the swollen shaft. "It's too early to start on that though. I don't want to be huge with a baby on our honeymoon."

"No, but it's like the run-up to the playoffs. We need to get in extra practice."

He took a condom from his pocket and handed it to me. "Is this how you fuck your groupies?" I asked as I put it on him. "You just take them in the hallways?"

"It's how I used to do it sometimes, but now you have an exclusive contract."

He lifted my leg and drove his hard prick into me, then grabbed the other leg and hoisted me up. As I hooked my heels around his waist he grabbed my ass cheeks cried out with pleasure as he impaled me with his thick, swollen cock. It felt incredibly hot as he slammed into me, driving me into the wall. He pinned my arms up over my head as he thrusted. My bad boy was taking me right there in the arena, fucking me hard, gloriously hard. With his cock moving inside me, the soft flesh of that massive prick massaged my flesh, arousing me. "Holy fuck," I heard myself moan.

My entire body clenched and the room spun. I came hard, almost violently.

"Damn, Chloe!" he moaned. "That's incredible."

I felt the pulsing of his cock inside me; he put his mouth to my neck and bit it as he came.

When he sighed softly, I kissed his cheek. "Damn right I'll marry you, Blake Collins."

18

BLAKE

It was hard to believe that the day had finally come. Who knew that I would end up being the type of guy to settle down with a woman I had fallen head over heels for, but it was real, and it had happened. In a blur of events Chloe and I had gotten married. I'd never been happier in my life, and she was the missing puzzle piece I never knew I needed until I found her. She fit perfectly in my life and was a great sidekick and groupie. I only needed her.

We'd been engaged six months, if you counted the pretend time and I still got a little tremor of lust every time I looked at her. Her warm inviting smile, intoxicating eyes and beautiful long blonde hair sent me over the edge of desire and I couldn't believe she was all mine. Her touch still aroused me instantly, and I found myself still not being able to get enough of her. Although I noticed other women, I had the one I wanted. She was always the hottest woman in every room she entered.

Even watching her dance with Tom Lassiter I couldn't help but be enchanted by her. She was spellbinding and mesmerized me.

"You know that this isn't very flattering," Daphne said. I was dancing with her and I looked down at her pretty face. "You have me here in your arms, up close and personal and you haven't been paying me any attention at all. A girl could get a complex."

"I'm sorry," I said, and chuckled.

She laughed. "It's kind of pathetic to see that the team's bad boy can't get his mind off his new wife for five minutes. Sweet, but pathetic."

"Chloe calls that being romantic. Who knew I could be that guy?" I laughed again.

Daphne touched my cheek. "She's right. It is and I'm teasing you mercilessly. How often do I get a chance to torment you, Blake? Of course, I must admit that Chloe is a smart, sexy, and very lucky woman."

I'd always liked Daphne. She was a nice kid. She seemed wise well beyond her years. "Well, she is smart and sexy anyway. I think I'm the lucky one."

"Damn right you are. And you better keep that in mind, because if you don't treat her right, I might have to kick your ass."

"I bet you could, too," I laughed. For a girl who'd just turned nineteen Daphne had a pretty good grasp of how things worked in the marriage department. I knew she would make some guy very lucky one day. "Seeing that I intend to worship her, I guess I don't have a thing to worry about."

"That's all out in the open then." She winked at me.

Tom and Chloe danced nearby and Daphne turned to her father. "Dance with me, Daddy. Blake is pining for his bride and being so saccharine about it I'm getting a toothache."

"Fine with me," Tom said. "I'll still get to have a lovely girl in my arms."

"You certainly will," I said, delighted to have Chloe

Fake Fiancé

floating back into my arms. I twirled her like the princess she was, looking at her graceful figure and knowing that she was perfect—everything I wanted in a life partner. Her white wedding gown was gorgeous, long and flowing with flowers and pearls decorating the bottom. She looked as if she walked right out of a fairy tale.

"I love you," she said. I felt my heart pounding. I'd never get tired of hearing that and it was wonderful to be loved. I didn't even know what I had been missing, but I knew that now I would never be able to live without her companionship. "Imagine, in twenty-four hours we'll be in Tahiti."

I couldn't stop envisioning Chloe in a smoking hot black bikini on the sand. I'd rub suntan oil all over her skin and watch her eyes heat with desire. Then I'd take her out into the surf, pull the little string to the side and fuck her wild as the waves rolled over us.

"I hope you haven't forgotten the evil intentions you promised to carry out." She pressed her curves to me with a smile and kissed my lips delicately, the ultimate tease in front of everyone.

"Not a one—they are all as evil as you can imagine." I grinned and she blushed.

She put her lips to my ear. "What are you going to do to me, husband?"

I practically growled as I pushed my hard length into her softness, making sure she knew exactly how badly I wanted her. "I'm going to fuck you on the beach and in the water. I'm going to keep you naked for a week and take you in every position." I dropped my hand to cup her ass and pulled her more tightly to me. "And everywhere. You're mine now, Chloe. All of you. And I have a very good imagination."

My cock throbbed as her soft lips tickling my neck. "I

love the way you think, my love, but all I hear is talk. I want some action."

"The way you inspire me, that shouldn't be a problem. You have a certain magic."

"Glad you noticed." She lightly and subtly let her hand graze the growing bulge in my pants. I was in for a lifetime of saucy fun with this delicious woman.

I doubted it would be possible for Chloe's magic to ever grow old for me. She had a wondrous lusty imagination when it came to our time together and I made sure I appreciated and savored every moment of it. I wasn't going to take advantage of our love. We had not known each other for very long, but the flame was burning strong within each of our hearts and the connection and chemistry had been instant. I never doubted for a moment that I had made the perfect choice to have Chloe as my bride.

EPILOGUE

BLAKE – ONE YEAR LATER

I paced the floor impatiently, ran my hands through my hair. I glanced out the window, scratched the stubble on my face. I couldn't hold still. I glanced at Chloe, who reached out a hand. I went over and took it, giving her hand a gentle squeeze. I was smiling at her as she lay on her back, her hand resting on her swollen belly.

"Relax," she said softly, smiling. "You're jittery and nervous when you have no reason to be. A big bad boy like you can handle this, can't you?" Her voice no doubt calmed me down a few notches; she had that patient demeanor that balanced me out whenever I needed it.

The feeling of her warm hand in mine calmed me. "If I really have to." I was only teasing her, I was just as eager as she was.

"Well, you'll have to. I don't think even a star hockey player can manage to speed things up." She continued to rub her belly.

Just then the doctor walked in the room, greeting Chloe first. She was a middle-aged lady with funky glasses and a bright, beaming smile. She saw me and stopped, staring. I knew she had recognized me.

Chloe chuckled. "Are you a hockey fan, Dr. Weiss?"

She blushed. "A Blizzards fan anyway. I try to make all the home games." Then she regained her composure and went back to her professional demeanor. I didn't mind, I loved it when I got recognized by a fan. Maybe I would autograph a puck for her or something. "But you're here for important business. Let's see how that baby is doing."

I watched as she uncovered Chloe's beautiful rounded belly, put jelly over a spot and pressed a sensor to it. The shadowy image came on the screen beside the bed and the sound of the baby's heartbeat filled the room, a strong pulsing sound. "That sounds healthy," I said. I felt instant relief rush over me, knowing my baby had a good strong heartbeat.

The doctor smiled at me. "A healthy heart and very good development." She paused. "Do you want to know the baby's sex?"

I looked at Chloe and she grinned. "It's your call, Blake. I already know."

"You know?" I was puzzled on how she found out. I couldn't help but feel a looming curiosity to know myself.

"A mother can tell."

The doctor shook her head. "They often think they know, but mothers are incredibly unreliable in that regard."

"Do you want to know, Blake?" Chloe asked me.

"Oh sure, why not," I grinned and sat up straighter.

"It's a girl."

I looked at the doctor. "Is it really?" I was beyond elated. The doctor nodded and smiled. "A healthy girl right on track for a full-term delivery." She looked at me again. "Both mother and baby seem right as rain."

I sighed and sank down into a chair. "Wow, this is great. Incredible really!"

A girl. Chloe and I were going to have a daughter. More importantly, I was going to be a father. Something I could have never even imagined a year ago. I was ready to take on the challenge and embrace a new role as husband, father, and protector.

"The receptionist will make an appointment for your next check-up, but I think this will be a simple delivery," the doctor said. She finished wiping Chloe's belly, pulled the gown back in place and started to leave.

"You should give the Doc a groupie shirt," Chloe teased, nudging me.

"You will never, ever, let me live that down." I shook my head but I knew she was kidding.

She grinned. "Why should I?"

"I can do better than that," I said. The doctor gave me a questioning look. "When you come to the season opener, give the usher your name. I'll arrange a seat for you in the owner's box." I stood up to shake the doctor's hand.

The woman's face lit up like a Christmas tree. "Wow! That would be great." Then she looked embarrassed. "Would it be possible to…"

"…bring a date? Sure. I'll arrange that. It would be my pleasure." I smiled at her, and I truly meant it. She was going to deliver my baby after all. I owed her that much.

As the door closed, Chloe laughed. "You can resist the girls but not being a macho bad boy."

"And you wouldn't want me to. It's part of the package remember?" I high-fived my beautiful, glowing wife.

"Not in the least…not when I'm getting the benefit of that bad, except for the tiny amount you use to flatten your opponents on the ice."

I let myself think about having a daughter, a tiny girl who

would grow up to be a beautiful and intelligent woman like her mother. I was excited to have a girl that I could bring out on the ice with me one day. Who knew, maybe she would have a flare and talent for skating. I loved dreaming about the future with both of my girls.

Chloe tried to sit up against the gravity of her growing belly so I offered her a hand in help. "Are you okay, Blake? You look worried. The doctor said everything is good." There was a hint of concern laced in that smooth voice of hers.

"We're having a daughter!" I exclaimed.

"So we all agree."

"She's never dating. And especially not an athlete." I was going to lay down the law before she was even born.

Chloe laughed. "Why not?"

"Because I know what men are like." I pointed to myself.

"So do I," she said. "We will bring her up to be a strong woman."

"Strong?" I didn't quite follow.

"Self-confident. Between us she will learn how to deal with people, hold her own and excel in everything she puts her mind to." She gave me a wicked smile. "I'll teach her how to keep those nasty boys in line. After all, someday she'll want one of her own."

That made me groan. I was ready to be a dad, but I was in no hurry to deal with other dicks out there. Though I knew it would come all too soon.

"Come on, Blake. She will be our little girl but then become her own woman—I know that's what you'll want for her. And you wouldn't want a son-in-law who was a wimp, would you?" Chloe got back into her regular clothes from the gown she had been wearing for the exam.

I wasn't so sure that wouldn't be exactly what I wanted. "It has a certain appeal." I didn't know why we had to worry about this *today*.

Fake Fiancé

Chloe laughed at me in her wonderful way that let me know I was being foolish. I was glad she found me cute.

"As long as it's not a guy like me." I hated to admit it, but my earlier bad boy days would live with me for a long time."

"I suppose we have time to discuss the issue of her dating."

"Let her get into grade school first," Chloe said, then we both chuckled.

I was overwhelmed by a flood of thoughts, dreams, concerns for this new life about to come into the world. I was dazed, off balance, and I'd never been happier, more content in my life.

Chloe looked up at me. "Kiss me, my bad boy."

"Gladly," I said and pulled her close and planned to never let her go.

ABOUT THE AUTHOR

Jessa James grew up on the East Coast but always suffered a severe case of wanderlust. She's lived in six states, had a variety of jobs and always comes back to her first true love – writing. Jessa works full time as a writer, eats too much dark chocolate, has an iced-coffee and Cheetos addiction, and can't get enough of sexy alpha males who know exactly what they want – and aren't afraid to say it. Dominant, alpha-male insta-luv is her favorite to read (and write).

Sign up HERE for Jessa's VIP Reader List
http://bit.ly/JessaJames

Connect with Jessa on Facebook:
http://bit.ly/JessaJamesFB

Jessa's Website:
http://jessajamesauthor.com

WANT MORE? READ HOW TO LOVE A COWBOY

Pete

I closed the ledger and leaned back into the rich cherry colored leather of the desk chair. I closed my eyes and rubbed my temples, thinking about how much easier things had been when my father was around running things at Killarny Estate. It wasn't anything I hadn't become accustomed to over the years. Being the oldest of the five Killarny brothers, it was expected from birth that I would be the one to take over the day to day running of the ranch. While all the brothers were equal partners in running the ranch, it was I who was the most responsible. Ask anyone. It was also me that my dad had turned to back when my mother, Emily Killarny, had first been diagnosed with breast cancer.

At my mother's request, I took on the additional tasks that my father had usually taken care of. Most of it was business, the sort of thing that didn't capture my attention quite like the quiet, meditative work with the horses, but I knew what had to be done. Most of all, I hadn't wanted to let my mother down.

Emily Killarny was a force unto herself, but she had a kind and good heart, and above all, she loved her children. I was aware that I had a special place in her heart when she had gone out of her way to be the best kind of grandmother she could be to Emma. I'd been dejected and alone, raising a two year old daughter alone after my ex-wife, Kelly, decided one day that motherhood and married life wasn't for her. My parents had been so kind to us in the days following that abandonment, and I would forever be grateful to both of them. My mother had especially done all that she could to make sure that Emma felt safe and loved after her mother's abrupt departure.

Back then my major responsibilities had been tending to the horses, something I still loved and wished I was able to do more of, but being the oldest, and since my father had relocated to Costa Rica, I knew I had to be the one to step up to the plate. My mother's death three years prior had taken a toll on the family patriarch, and after suffering a severe bout of depression, he finally decided to make some major changes. One of those changes included leaving the states and relocating to a warmer climate, leaving the green Kentucky hills behind him in favor of sun and sand. Some days I couldn't help but feel a little jealous of that, but I knew that my heart would always be right here, wherever Emma was.

I opened my eyes again and looked at my computer screen for a moment before getting up and heading for the door, grabbing my jacket on the way. There was still a chill in the air that early in the Kentucky spring and it was invigorating to step out into the morning air, breathing in the fresh smell of new grass and the less pleasing scent wafting from the nearest barn. The smell of manure might not have appealed to everyone, but for me, it was a reminder of home and childhood.

I breathed in the air and made my way over to the stables where my brother Alex was brushing out the coat of a two year old mare.

"She looks beautiful," I said as I came up to stand on the other side of the stall door.

Alex nodded. "Siobhan is quite a looker." He brushed her russet coat to a glistening sheen that caught the early morning sun and made the horse look like a copper penny.

"You think we'll run her next year?" I asked him as I looked over the horse from nose to tail. She was beautiful, but I wasn't sure if she was one of the horses that we would end up taking to the many derbies we were involved in.

Alex shrugged. "Not sure. She hasn't been run that much, and I really think that if we had planned on doing that with her, she should have seen a little more practice at this point in her life. I think she is a great horse, but I'm not sure the derby life is the one for her. However, I do think she is going to give us a lot of talented foals."

Alex was probably the quietest of all the brothers, so hearing him talk this much was a little unusual. The only time Alex had much to say was when he was talking about a horse. Not much for words and usually keeping to himself, he was definitely the most horse whisperer like among us and was more involved with the training of individuals here at the ranch. He was so in tune with the horses that it helped to have his expertise around to help people become accustomed to green horses. While most of our horses were bred here on the ranch, we did keep a group of wild ponies from the Dakotas on one of the spreads of land that was fenced off from the rest. Alex's house was out there and visiting that part of the ranch felt like entering a wilderness. I could see why my parents had given him that parcel when they were divvying up the land to us. It fit my younger brother's personality perfectly, and he was never happier than he was when he was among the wild horses.

"Her mother is Spring, right?" I asked.

"Yeah, and her father was David's Lariat."

David's Lariat had been one of Alex's favorites. A horse that my father had acquired from a Colorado ranch when we were still very young, the horse had been a monster of an animal when we got him. He stood taller than any of our other horses but managed to be faster than almost any horse half his weight. He was a marvel and had produced many of our fastest horses. David's Lariat had died just a year before, but we still had a few of his offspring around the ranch and would likely see his influence in our derby horses for decades to come.

"Well, even if she isn't going to run for us, she's a beautiful girl, and I'm sure she'll give us a few great runners."

"What are you up to?" Alex asked as he put away the brush and stepped out of the stall to join me where I stood.

I shrugged. "Just needed to get out of the office for a little while."

"Already?" He looked at his watch. "It's early in the day. Why don't you hire someone to take care of some of the stuff you don't enjoy? That's what bookkeepers are for, after all. It would give you a break and let you have a chance to get back out here with the horses where you want to be."

Alex was perceptive with more than just the horses.

"Yeah, well, I might do that after the next couple of derbies have passed. I've got too much on my plate right now to hand it over to someone totally new."

My brother sighed and shrugged. "Whatever you say. Just don't be afraid to ask for a little help when you need it."

I gave him a firm pat on the back and continued on down through the stables, past the stalls that housed our many horses. A few of our ranch hands were leading some of the horses out to graze in the pasture, while some of them were headed to the arena and our track for training. As I exited the other end of the massive stable, I saw Emma atop her horse, Saoirse.

"How'dya do, Miss Emma Lou?"

Emma frowned at me, and I could see her brow furrowing under her helmet. I knew she hated it when I referred to her middle name, Louise, but told myself that someday she would come to think of it as endearing, so I kept up the practice.

She tossed her head back. "Saoirse and I just went out for our morning run. I was about to take her back to the stable and then head in for my lessons. Is Hetty here yet?"

I shook my head. "She wasn't there when I left the house, but there's a good chance she's arrived by now. Better hurry on back, you don't want to be late."

My twelve year old daughter beamed at me from where she sat on her horse and headed into the stable before dismounting. I watched her lead her young horse into the stall and couldn't help but notice how much she was starting to look like her mother. It wasn't a bad thing, but I did wonder how Emma would feel as she looked in the mirror and started to notice the resemblance she shared with the woman who left her—and me—behind when Emma was just a toddler.

I walked toward the pasture as I recalled the time directly after Kelly left. It had been a shock to me when it happened, but when I had a little time to think it over, nothing about it was too surprising. We had married straight out of high school, and my parents had been opposed to the match from the start. Kelly's parents were business owners in the nearest town, and ours had been the kind of wedding that made the local papers. Our courtship had been brief — we dated at the end of high school, and because I was an idiot, I had proposed to Kelly not long after graduation. We married and moved into a house here at Killarny Estate and had had a hell of a time for the first couple of years.

Kelly was wild and looking back I could tell she had been just a little too wild for me. It wasn't something I had noticed at the time, and while it was just the two of us, it was easy to forget that we were stepping into a new world that included all sorts of new responsibilities. Back then we would spend our weekends hopping around the bars in town before heading back to the privacy of our house at the ranch and going at it like rabbits. It was no surprise when Kelly got pregnant, and I was overjoyed, but she didn't seem too enthused about it. Slowly she warmed to the idea, and once Emma was born, I could see that she really did love our daughter.

Things were never the same though. Kelly never looked at me the same way, and I tried to encourage her to go see a doctor to see if what she was struggling with was postpartum depression, but she wouldn't listen.

I came home one evening to find all of Kelly's things gone, a note on the kitchen table, and Emma wailing in her playpen. I had picked up my daughter and the note and read the words through tears as Emma sniffled and buried her head against my shoulder. Kelly was gone. She apologized in the letter, said she was heading to California to pursue her dream of being an actress, and that she was going with her friend, Bud.

Bud was the guy she had dated before me in high school, and suddenly it all started to make sense. We never really heard from her after that, aside from a Christmas card or a birthday present for Emma on the years that Kelly remembered, which were few and far between.

As far as I knew, Emma had no real memory of her

Want more? Read How To Love A Cowboy

mother. It made me sad, but I wondered if it was for the best that she didn't know what she was missing out on. If Kelly had hung around much longer, it would have been more difficult than it already was to get Emma used to not having her mother around.

I had been so grateful to my parents for the support they were during that time, especially my mother. She had done all she could to be the maternal figure in my daughter's life, but she never stopped pressing me to go on dates and get out there again, constantly reminding me that I was still young and there was happiness out there for me if I would just go looking for it.

Her last attempt had been just a few years before she passed away when I had first hired Hetty Blackburn, a local teacher, to be Emma's tutor. The ranch was well out of the way, and it was quite a hike to the nearest school, so I had decided to homeschool Emma. It gave her a chance to be around the horses more and to study at her own pace, which was quite a bit faster than the average elementary school student, according to Hetty.

Hetty was pretty and a very sweet woman. Her black hair and blue eyes were a sort of bewitching combination that was hard to ignore, but I couldn't get back into dating; not then and not now, even though it was 10 years since Kelly walked out. Even if I hadn't already been very hesitant to date, Hetty already had one major strike against her—she knew my daughter.

I leaned against the bright white fence and watched as a group of our horses played together in the dewy field that was filled with clover. The place was even more picturesque than usual in this light. Killarny Estate was really something to be proud of, and I was so glad to have the privilege of being a part of a four generation horse ranch, the largest one in Kentucky, and now, for all intents and purposes, running the place.

One rule I had established for myself was that until I knew I could trust a woman, she would never meet my daughter. And since I wasn't in the mood to start dating yet, nothing had ever made it that far. Sure, I had been with women since Kelly—too many to count—but I was there to get what I wanted and get out. I never went out with anyone that I thought was there for more than what I was because I had more heart than that. But I didn't trust anyone to give me any more than what I was looking for at the moment. It was sex, pure and simple—though rarely pure or simple. I was there for a release, to have sex, hear them scream my name, and then leave quietly. The closest I had ever come to bringing a woman home was the Lawrence girl who I made it all the way back to the ranch with, but we never left my truck. We had made it as far as the pecan grove when I pulled over and had her right there in the cab of my pickup. When we were done, I turned around and drove her right back to her house. But that had been the last one, and that had been a long time ago now.

There was no need to complicate my life any more than it already was and I was certainly not going to bring any of these women into the life of my daughter. She had already experienced enough pain from my poor choices, and I wasn't going to do that to her again.

My middle brother, Jake, came riding up on his stallion and brought the horse to a quick halt a few feet away from me.

"Showing off?" I asked as I cocked my eyebrow at him.

He swung down off the saddle and gave the horse a pat. "This bastard is ready to run!"

Clement certainly looked like he was ready for it. His eyes

Want more? Read How To Love A Cowboy

were wild, but it was clear that he was happy after his morning run with Jake.

"Think about how fast he's going to be with one of the jockeys on him!"

I nodded. "We're taking him to the Waters derby, right?"

"Yup, just a couple of weeks away now."

I noted to myself that I needed to check that out on the calendar. There was still a lot left to do in preparation, and we weren't sure how many horses we would be taking. Clement was certainly on the top of the list, but I knew we needed to have a few backups. Killarny Estate had always been top of the pack as far as producing some of the fastest race horses in the country, but ever since my father had packed it up and gone to Costa Rica, it felt like we had lost some of our edge. I had no idea what it was Dad had that we didn't quite have down yet, other than the forty years of experience. What I did know was that it was crucial for us to win this derby. Things were tight, and if we were going to turn them around and maintain things the way they were around here, or if we were ever going to have any hope of making Killarny the very best again, we had to win the Waters derby.

"You coming?" Jake asked me as he brushed his reddish-brown hair back out of his face and wiped his brow with the back of his sleeve.

I looked at him bewildered. "Of course I am."

He shrugged. "Don't act like it's a given. You haven't been there in years."

"Yeah, well…now I don't really have any choice, do I? Dad is still in Costa Rica, and I don't know the next time he's planning on coming back, so I've got to be there to represent the ranch. And I think Emma would enjoy the trip to Tennessee, so yeah, I'll be there."

Want more? Read How To Love A Cowboy

"You're not nervous, are you?" Jake winked at me, and I frowned in response.

"Why would I be nervous?"

"Because," he began, pausing to spit on the ground. "Little Sara Waters is going to be there. I wonder if she is going to follow you around like she always used to when we were kids."

I rolled my eyes. "Sara Waters is thirty by now. I am sure she has got better things to do than chase around a nearly middle-aged man with his twelve year old daughter in tow."

"Hey now, don't write yourself off just yet. You're only a year or so older than her, right? I bet she would be champing at the bit to get a piece of a Killarny brother."

I shook my head and started off back toward the stable, Jake following behind me with Clement.

"Then she can have her pick of the other four. Hell, she can have both Stephen and Sam if she wants them." I stopped and looked around. "Speaking of that, where are the twins?"

Jake shrugged as he continued toward the stable. "Who the hell knows. They're out every night of the week. Probably still in bed."

I knew he was kidding about the last thing. If we had been taught anything as kids, it was that getting up early in the morning was the Killarny way.

"Okay, well. I need to go find them. I'll get back to you about the Waters derby. We need to talk about some logistics getting there, but it can wait until later."

As I walked off toward the other barns to locate my two youngest brothers, I couldn't help thinking about what Jake had said regarding Sara Waters. I hadn't seen her since we were practically teenagers. It must have been a decade or so. I wondered what she looked like now and if there was a chance that we'd get some time alone when I was at her father's derby in a few weeks.

GET A FREE BOOK!

Join my mailing list to be the first to know of new releases, free books, special prices and other author giveaways.

http://freehotcontemporary.com

JESSA JAMES BOOKS

Bad Boy Billionaires
Lip Service
Rock Me
Lumberjacked
Baby Daddy

The Virgin Pact
The Teacher and the Virgin
His Virgin Nanny
His Dirty Virgin

Club V
Unravel
Undone
Uncover

Beg Me
Valentine Ever After

www.ingramcontent.com/pod-product-compliance
Lightning Source LLC
LaVergne TN
LVHW011842060526
838200LV00054B/4132